# LEGEND OF THE MIGHTY SPARROW,
## PART 3

END OF DAYS, ESCHATOLOGY, THE FINAL
EVENTS OF HISTORY, THE ULTIMATE
HUMAN DESTINY, END OF TIME, AND
ULTIMATE FATE OF THE UNIVERSE

## BRYAN FLETCHER

authorHOUSE®

*AuthorHouse™*
*1663 Liberty Drive*
*Bloomington, IN 47403*
*www.authorhouse.com*
*Phone: 1 (800) 839-8640*

*Published by AuthorHouse   11/15/2016*

*ISBN: 978-1-5246-4980-7 (sc)*
*ISBN: 978-1-5246-4978-4 (hc)*
*ISBN: 978-1-5246-4979-1 (e)*

*Library of Congress Control Number: 2016919030*

*Print information available on the last page.*

*Any people depicted in stock imagery provided by Thinkstock are models, and such images are being used for illustrative purposes only.*
*Certain stock imagery* © *Thinkstock.*

*This book is printed on acid-free paper.*

*For more information about the Legend of the Mighty Sparrow series visit http://legendofthemightysparrow.com/ or bfletch157@yahoo.com, Facebook.*

# CHAPTER 1

In an ultradense forest, which proves difficult to see five feet ahead, Bonnie struggles through, and behind her, the dog follows at a safe distance, which irritates her to no end, so she feints to drive it off, yet to no avail, then chases it off with a clinically insane surge, an eight-step-go-away-surge with wild arm actions.

However, after the last step, she hears something, and quietly plows towards then finds a nearby stream.

Yet as she turns away, something catches her eye, so she moves closer for a better look, as a fish takes a mighty leap, then another feisty flop.

"Oh my, fish sticks, or fish and chips!" she duly claims, which causes her to perk up, and the stomach votes then whole body unanimously ratifies, with no dissenting votes, not even that pesky moral thing, that little voice, the one that knows how to burrow deep inside the psyche, to pester and peck from the best possible angles, and just at the right time to make a point, to gets its way.

After squeezing through dense brush, she discards a borrowed small foreign diplomatic sack with straps, one that smells of frogs, which move inside, inside various plastic bags.

And Bonnie considers methods to catch fish, as they seem a more reasonable meal compared to frogs, more civilized, "Yes," then she constructs a fish gaff, a long stick with sharp hook on the end, such as a broken branch junction that extends several inches, yet remains sharp, which represents simplicity at its best, and one of the first prehistoric tools.

And of equal importance, it quickly constructs, seems easy to use, well, in theory: just slowly ease it into the water at the proper angle, and account for the prism effect, then approach as another fish might, from the side with a calm respect, which has a life application, then once next to a fish, and with a rapid jerk, snag it from underneath or the gill and fling it out of the water.

All the while, the dog watches with fascination.

However, after standing in cold water for thirty minutes, and a considerable number of failed attempts, stumbles, and one clumsy belly flop after another, she realizes the difficulty, as creeping up, easing a stick into the water, maneuvering it under the fish, and that clean jerk motion proves tricky, quite.

So much so, she eventually tires and simply flops down in the water, as the dog carefully studies.

Moments later, she cautiously looks around for danger, and at one angle after another, as well as listens then exits the water, and a stubborn personality emerges, very much so, an obsession, of frustration, agitation, and mumble of words not in the dictionary then words not fit for print.

As a result, she expends a great deal of effort constructing a barb-tipped spear, which misses, again and again, as it might not represent the correct angle.

Then after constructing a trident and, jabbing here and there, it catches nothing.

And all as frustration continues to build.

"No fishing pole, line, hook or reel.

"I want those fish sticks."

And because of dismay, Bonnie plops in the water, sits, and considers.

However, something else happens, something.

For a few moments, time or the temporal inflection distorts, yet she ignores and daydreams about fish sticks, the number that could and should be eaten in one sitting, and all the ways to enjoy them, especially "with ketchup or tartar sauce, yes," as well as "How many fish sticks can fit in the mouth at the same time?

"I want those fish sticks."

Moments later, an idea arrives, and regardless of danger, the real possibility of snakes, as they prefer that location type, that position to nip.

# CHAPTER 2

As a result, she sets homemade equipment aside then wades through thick water brush and finds a deeper section, one with a considerable enclave, where a person can quickly ventilate, hold a deep breath, then explore with a dive.

Which she does, yet seems unable to look inside the poorly lit hole for fish sticks, and with a strained reach inside feels around, and again regardless of the prime snake habitat.

Just as significantly, stubbornness does that: it can suspend the ability to reason, suspend logic.

And still unable to see inside, she rises, quickly ventilates several times, holds a deep breath, goes under then reaches inside and feels around for fish sticks, and explores the entire area for well over a minute.

Empty.

In addition, this hole does not have a snake, such as a water moccasin, also known as a cottonmouth, and not even a northern copperhead, or timber rattlesnake, "Yes," to grab one mid strike, mid leap with fangs.

Regardless, she tries again, feels around, as it seems vital to feel around the murky water, touch then with a fast reflex, grab one by the head.

And how difficult could it be to grab a snake mid nip?

Empty.

So, she rises, breathes, then moves to one murky section after the other, where the head can barely remain above water then arm reaches inside a passage and feels around.

# CHAPTER 3

"Yes, something is in this one, maybe a snake; something big—very big," and Bonnie strains.

Then it bites her hand, which causes her to reel a great distance, and eventually her demeanor changes to wholly determined, as well as fully possessed.

"Maybe a snake, beaver or muskrat is in there, as it happened so fast," which shows as complete astonishment, and how could something strike that fast?

Yet she carefully returns, and reaches inside, further, and around then strains.

Moments later, it bites, and she reels back to a serious distance, and flabbergasts for some time then carefully considers the damage, the bite marks in great detail, then she shows a demonic smile, of true clinical insanity, yes, then sticks her arm back in that murky hole and fully extends, reaches, strains and reaches further.

As a result, it bites again, which causes eyes to widen beyond reason.

However, the stubborn thought of fish sticks, and tartar sauce, yes, causes her to reach even deeper.

Moments later, a violent struggle begins, which causes her body to alternate between violent shakes, tremendous reels, then total chaos.

# CHAPTER

Eventually, she staggers out of the water, and onto the stream bank with a huge catfish, which has swallowed her entire hand, and it takes a while as well as considerable persuasion to remove, such as an ever so wild action of swinging here and there, something a person might not want on YouTube, well, as it might earn a certain unfortunate reputation.

However, it eventually releases then flops about.

And this reveals a hand and arm with serious cuts, wounds and abrasions, things most people might become hysterical, then run about, as well as rant and rave until, that person eventually passes out, the style where feet fly high in the air, another YouTube moment, a situation likely to earn many clicks, and enough so, well, to crowd out nightly news, serious news, such as real relief, and not the manufactured news created by powerful interests, too-big-to-fail, such as to sell crispy bacon or some other product, such as a path into another quagmire, or keep digging in the traditional quagmire, and a YouTube moment to crowd out vital subjects to the human species, to the history of.

Regardless, Bonnie reenters the water and looks for another one, in another hole, and really digs about in the murky water then feels something, "Yes," and soon struggles, then as if a true maniac.

Moments later, something bites her, and again, which causes her to reel a great distance, then her demeanor changes to wholly determined, as well as fully possessed about a profound subject, "Maybe a snake, beaver or muskrat, yes, is inside, as it happened so fast.

"And how could something strike that fast?"

Yet she carefully returns, and reaches further inside, reaches around then strains.

Moments later, it bites and she seriously reels back a great distance then flabbergasts, for some time, and carefully considers the damage, considers all those bite marks in great detail, then she shows a demonic smile, of clinical insanity then sticks her arm back in that murky hole and fully extends, reaches, strains and reaches further and hooks the hand around the gills, then drags it ashore.

"Fish sticks, yes!"

"I'll clean, dry, and smoke the fish," then she notices the borrowed small foreign diplomatic sack with straps, one that smells of frogs, which move inside various plastic bags.

"Oh, and frog legs."

However, she needs a safe place.

So she travels a considerable distance, mostly west, and all the while carefully listens as well as looks about for danger at various angles, and eventually locates a safe place; yet making a fire might prove difficult, especially because of that previous rain, the dampness.

However, a fire option exists, the char cloth, with cloth easily combustible, and made from a previous campfire, then stored inside her backpack, in that small four-ounce tin can with lid.

However, the cloth needs a spark, a source.

She has none, which causes a serious frown.

Yet moments later, an idea arrives, and she hunts for two rocks, for just the right types, which proves quite difficult to find, and in a way that does not attract attention from those bears.

And the process eventually requires a rock bash, a repeated bashing of rocks against one another, for a spark.

Then she remembers that last bear encounter, the foam, and that ever so disgusting thick white foam which dripped from the bear mouth onto the jaw, fur, ground, and her hands, which causes her to again wipe both hands beyond rhythm or reason.

Eventually, she snaps out of that mindset and digs for more rocks then tests one after another, yet none neatly split into smaller and more a manageable pieces, or functions, such as to produce a blade, a sliver or spark, a flint action.

So, char cloth is not an option, at least for now.

Instead, she digs inside the backpack, retrieves a previously constructed bow drill fire making set, which did not work before, and she remembers cursing like a sailor.

Maybe one of the components was moisture, the drill stick, softwood slotted board or tinder, and she touches each to her face then says, "They feel dry, or dry enough."

However, that small amount of emergency tinder would burn for maybe thirty seconds.

As a result, she quietly gathers dry kindling, tests against the cheek, and often stops then eyes carefully scan for obvious as well as subtle forest aspects one section at a time.

Then eyes widen, nostrils flare, as she waits motionless and without expression then ever so slowly scans the area as eyes narrow and search for obvious as well as subtle things, section by section, including above and below yet not behind, then scans for context, especially stagecraft, theatrical cues, show controls and a playwright-associated metathetic.

# CHAPTER 5

Eventually Bonnie sits and eats smoked catfish, as well as roasted acorns, worms, grubs, ants, various roots, strips of roasted pine bark, and occasionally sips on pine needle tea brewed in a tin can.

In fact, she seems quite pleased, as well as a bit playful then thoughts turn to later, dinner plans, and a novel idea, stew made with dried bark as a flour substitute.

However, she stops chewing on pine bark, more like chopping, and says, "Wait a minute.

"Hold the freakin' horses," then stares at the dog, really stares.

"I've never seen you eat, ever, and yet you look well-fed.

"Just as importantly, I offer food, yet each time you show no interest and give me the no-way look, as if it represents a caveman meal."

Another realization brightens then she says, "Now I remember, you only eat homemade dog food with those complex recipes, that ultimate gourmet stuff.

"Yes, that list contained eight pages of recipes and was attached to the mansion property agreement, as terms of sale when Agrippa bought the mansion. And it contained step-by-step instructions on how to make highfalutin dog food, as well as other mandates, such as take you on a three-mile walk each day, then before bedtime read literature to you, from a predetermined list, which also included *Grimms' Fairy Tales*, *The Grapes of Wrath* by John Steinbeck, *David Copperfield* by Charles Dickens, *I, Claudius* by Robert Graves, *1984* by George Orwell, and if you got really bored, then read *Finnegans Wake* by James

Joyce, or from those other books, yes, from the lower mansion library bookshelf.

"Yes, now I remember."

Then with suspicion, Bonnie stares at the dog and puts aside her meal and says, "Come closer" as crumbs roll down her shirt, which causes the dog to show one puzzled head movement after another.

"Yes, you, come closer.

"Now!"

And the dog edges slightly forward.

"No, further.

"More."

Then she takes a very close look at the dog, then from a series of front angles, side, back and top.

"What the hell?

"What kind of dog is this?"

And the dog intently looks, listens then does a neat backflip, a deliberately slow high arc that takes it well over five feet in the air.

Next, it does a quick tight backflip, barely off the ground.

Then quite pleased with itself, it hops about as if a four-legged kangaroo, with high bounces here and there then stops yet the tail wags satisfaction.

As a result, she says slowly, "What the hell?"

Then the dog practices a series of ultrafast dart and pivot skills, then bounces high off one tree after another and finishes by neatly climbing one tree after another then returns and lies down with tongue a-hanging.

There it pants.

"Really?

"And every night you disappear.

"Let me guess: you take a nightly constitutional and you don't eat?

"Come closer.

"Yes, you, come closer, now."

And the dog edges forward.

"Further."

And she considers it then reexamines the dog collar tag for details, which has an elaborate inscription, *MY NAME IS DOG. YES, SIMPLY CALL ME DOG, AND SAY IT WITH WILD EYES, EXAGGERATED GUSTO, OR SAY IT WITH HANDS EXTENDED OUT, PALMS UP TOWARD THE HEAVENS, AND HANDS AS IF CLAWS THEN SHAKE THEM WITH REAL STYLE, OR SAY IN A VERY LOUD VOICE, AS IF YOU'RE A MISSION COMMANDER, SUCH AS TO KICKASS, OR PUT ANOTHER WAY, AS IF YOU'RE IN A MOOD TO KICKASS AND TAKE NAMES!*

Just as importantly, Bonnie smells something, so she sniffs about, looks, sniffs and cranes closer to it.

"Moon pies!

"You've eaten moon pies?

"Yes, you did; orange—an orange double decker. Orange only comes in a double decker.

"Okay, you now have my full attention.

"Show me the moon pies."

No reaction.

Then Bonnie says in a full command voice, "Take me to the moon pies!"

As a result, the dog snaps to attention, turns, and travels essentially west through ultradense forest, which she follows, and this strange and exceptionally complex path has few straight lines, many pauses, lots of belly crawling, moving atop obstacles and through what seems impenetrable.

Finally after traveling a great distance, all the while having to strain, stretch, scrap through, bend, shimmy, climb, leap over, slip around, deflect, zigzag once too often, she calls for the dog to stop.

"Wait, why not shortcut through here or there, yes, there?"

The dog looks and shakes a refusal, then points ever so true to this and that, which she does not see.

Then it continues that complex route, which causes her to grumble and eventually give up the shortcut idea, and instead autopilots based on his lead.

Within hours, the dog stops and wags at a heavily overgrown area, then digs through overgrowth, which reveals a house foundation, as well as huge marks that give the full impressive something massive rudely gouged out the above ground aspects.

And further west sits a few more examples covered with dense overgrowth, as each removed house appears to have been over 9,000 square feet and sat on their own large plot of land.

Then the dog digs at one location after another, which reveals a pile of rubble that includes elegant furniture, such as a dresser and kitchen cabinets, and all of them show exquisite craft.

Eventually, the dog uncovers more household rubble and construction supplies that include a rocking chair, vintage Schwinn Green Hornet bicycle, car battery, eleven-gallon galvanized steel washtub, red union suit with a backdoor flap, a custom pasta maker monogramed with the initials JM, and off to the side sits a small wooden bed, which might remind a person of *Forrest Bed, The Architect's Brother*.

They also find a few car parts, such as for a Bentley Continental Flying Spur, Rolls Royce Phantom, Lamborghini Murciélago, Joss Supercar, Mercedes-Benz S-Class, as well as PVC pipe, Saran Wrap, car battery, components to make cement, and she finds two green plastic five-ounce spray bottles, as well as a one-of-a-kind Fender Strat electric guitar with a small rickety old-style amp.

And off to the side sits a bathtub, one similar to the *Herbeau* Creations *Medicis* with weathered polished copper and pewter, yet this one has more upscale features, especially the faucets, and it stands on a rare *Paradiso* Bash marble base and is filled with rainwater.

Then she sniffs about and says, "Yes, I need a bath"

"However, where are those moon pies?"

So she digs underneath more thick growth and finds an elegant hardwood cabinet with world-class details. And the doors have full-length piano-style hinges and open to show a jaw-dropping collection of premium liquor as well as stemware, in fact worldclass.

And this cabinet has two dovetail-constructed drawers with smooth running metal slides, which provide utensil storage and include shelves that extend as work surfaces, to mix drinks or prepare something extra, maybe a snack, a canapé, an *hors d'oeuvre*, such as puff pastry, or a cracker, yes, topped with a savory or two, and eaten in one bite, yes.

Then she looks through the utensil drawers and only finds a corkscrew, yet a second look reveals something hidden in the back, a high-end leather suitcase, remarkable in fact, which she opens and finds skimpy fantasy costumes, super sexy ones, such as a wild cowgirl with considerable whip, sly French maid, incorruptible cop, demanding pirate, perky head cheerleader, innocent Miss Bunny, as well as an eager-to-serve sailor on leave.

"I see, a sexy lady.

Regardless, where are the moon pies?"

Then she turns and digs elsewhere in dense foliage for food, then remembers the kitchen cabinets and beelines for them.

And inside one after another sits a wide variety of worldclass canned goods, pasta and spices, especially various gourmet chili powders, as well as an atomic or two, such as *Bhut Jolokia*, then after opening another set of cabinets, and in magnificent glory, moon pies!

In fact, they contain a case of every possible flavor, well, nearly, even ones that never made it to the marketplace, the type reserved for special clients, for people in the know, for insiders with gravitas.

As a result her jaw drops and eyes widen.

"Holy smokes, mother of all creatures great and small!

"This is absolutely magnificent," and she beams, admires, fawns over in great detail, takes a meticulous inventory, percolates all the while, then notices expiration dates and seriously ponders yet eventually shrugs, "It could be worse."

And both of them eat and eat.

"Now, that's stupid good."

All the while, she devours and makes all types of inarticulate sounds that convey consideration, satisfaction, and joy then often, a considerable pause, to breathe, which only seems natural.

Then a better idea arrives: why not bathe and eat at the same time?

And after a careful survey in all directions for danger, even crouching at one angle after another for a better view, she gathers an armful of food and the most expensive booze then arranges them near the tub, within arm's reach.

And a naughty smile emerges.

So much so, she playful stripteases for some imaginary person, and her hips move in a way that reveals her curves, shows a full invitation and offers delight, as well as a possibility.

Then she blows gentle kisses, and lips pout, flirt as well as a wink beckons, as one piece of clothing slides off after another and reveals her magnificent curves.

In fact, she playfully arches her back to reveal more curves, then offers them, and practices one wardrobe malfunction after another, practices various routines, such as oops, and ever so innocent then Marilyn Monroe imitations, and playfully bats eyes, flirts, tosses hair, then shows an ever so long leg, oh my.

And one after another, she reveals her Victoria secrets, and each time shows a magnificent curve as well as better view.

Then she playfully twirls a garment in the air, and eventually cast a seductive spell, a poetic truth, both obvious and subtle, yes, a spell to bring you closer and closer.

"Can you see my curves?

"Do you want to see more?"

# CHAPTER 6

All the while in comprehensive stealth, a boulder creature, similar to *Star Trek: The Savage Curtain* smolders, shifts, duly notes then looks toward the serene blue expanse of sky, to the heavens, and really studies something beyond the Sloan Great Wall, then Giant Void in NGH, then turns slightly.

Somehow, that enables it to observe a meeting elsewhere, hundreds of miles away in Washington, DC, as Gus, that same minor congressional aide from the ill-fated mansion fundraiser, travels along one long hallway after another then eventually enters a considerable ad hoc meeting in progress, which contains congressional committee members, discreet aides, power brokers, special interest factions, and foils for the shadow. And all of them except Gus often look over their shoulders and down the hallway before speaking, to ensure complete privacy, then they collectively decide to enter a nearby small nondescript office, with no nameplate or any sign of status, and a place less likely to be known by competitors, reporters or allies, whether they be direct or indirect, and more importantly, a place less likely to be bugged by each other or various aspects of the great umpteen.

Still in full stealth, that rock creature continues to smolder, shift, often turn and explain to someone else, yet no one else sits inside that space, in what may be an isolated subspace domain, or impluvium of sorts, yet a place that gives the full impression of a portable aedicula paradox, a temporal exception.

However, a closer inspection implies the creature speaks to another place, another world, as if through an exceptionally small gunk, and not the commercial version within the brain, which has all that mental chatter, clamor, crush of "Buy now— yes, now," as well as clatter, clang and contradiction, such as a can-can dance.

It transmits data through a nearby phenomenon, as in the very serious physics and topology associated with gunk.

Although this may be an accurate description, an even closer inspection suggests something else, and not a high-speed data transmission through quantum entanglement, and of how all things seem connected even over vast distances, such as light-years away. Where, things might theoretically replicate over vast distances in an instant, a transporter if you will, not that.

However, an even more detailed look at this creature communications system implies it uses part of the universal container itself, and aspects of the universe that exists everywhere, even when matter does not exist in a given location, for example a void or a great expanse of nothing, and this communication system has something to do with Euclidean space, which has time and space coordinates, such as the International Celestial Reference Frame. And yet somehow it also relates to matter and life. How they orient and have a preference in time and space, which for a human includes anatomical planes for instance coronal, transverse, sagittal and parasagittal; these four orientations also go by frontal, horizontal, lateral and parasagittal planes, and of equal importance, all of which according to this creature system, seem to give things and even the lack of things a mobile address within the universe, in relation to the supreme bulkhead, or supreme stack, the universe with transverse and longitude supports, and more than walls within a ship hull or fuselage that partition elements, or the metaverse, multiverse, metastack or meta-stash.

Then the boulder creature turns slightly, yet that allows a meeting observation thousands of miles away, of a patrician standing into a control room, filled with staff who monitor financial day traders at an elaborate bank of flat screen monitors, which show real-time stocks, stock options, currencies and futures contracts, such as equity index, interest rate, and commodity.

Just as importantly, each screen rapidly updates the latest information for his European bank, with a longstanding patrician-class affiliation and fast proximal server.

Then clearly engaged, the patrician exits the room and travels a series of hallways in his German garden-mansion, and one quite similar to *Grüneburgschlößchen*, Frankfurt, one of the many Rothschild-style mansions, and not a Gilded Age version, the nouveau riche, yet this one has many features a person might expect in a secular temple, if you will, or tome, a sacred precinct with special rules, and surrounded by an extraordinary forty-acre garden, in fact a picturesque place of colorful bloom, which includes shrubs, subshrubs, and special herbal plants, yet not a virtuous treatise of medicinal, tonic, culinary and aromatic expressions, nevertheless what one might expect within the golden age of classical and Renaissance gardens.

Eventually, the German patrician reaches for the doorknob, notices something, stops, and waits without motion.

Then something happens, something.

However, it becomes more specific, yet not within sight, and it has a certain feel of a PowerShell, a transhuman, posthuman, and yet a WS-Trust hypnagogia, with a transitional state from wakefulness to sleep, yet a walled Accumulo NoSQL garden if you will.

As a result, his eyes widen and nostrils flare, then he slowly scans the entire area, as eyes narrow and search for obvious and subtle things.

Yet everything now seems normal and in the correct place.

So, he reaches for that same doorknob then midway freezes, and waits, and really waits, as if in an *iānuae* threshold, a well-known port, or well-known binary, and carefully scans in a way that shifts back and forth, from questioning to studious of the smallest details, and all done without blinking—as the eyes often narrow and methodically scan section-by-section, even above, below, yet not behind.

Eventually, he carefully backsteps to gain safety, and further, then once at a considerable distance and out of that field or event horizon, scans the area, as if a scout at the frontier.

However, nothing seems out of the ordinary. Nothing, and the nose takes a few cautious samples and the mind considers all evidence, as well as what might seem trivial.

Then as he nears that door and reaches out, things darken around the periphery then remind this person of living in a cave, in a very familiar place, a place-based education, of primes and unusual places, possibly Plato's cave or some mystic grotto, and one that seems ancient, oddly illuminated, and more important, a telling, or teller of an election, amendment or possibly a dangerous mine, which a pioneer might dig at the substratum, or search for a Bethany-style solution, yet finds procrastination, the self and crucial syncretism sparks, of *verbum sat zapienti est*, to rise from the rut, rise.

And moments later, this German patrician frequently experiences a sense of tremendous awe, which causes mouth and eyes to widen, as this person quickly looks for AB hylomorphs, for Franz Kafka notions, Schröder–Bernstein theorem of measurable space, indexicality, as well as human aspects, and not in a conventional sense of the body, mind and soul, for instance, something you might find near a very specific well of souls, and that phase transition not easily quantifiable.

All of which causes a strange and extraordinary thrill, a marvel, as well as mystery, which shows on the face, and the internal body alarm warns of exceptional frontier danger, and yet, as if at a threshold of sheer greatness, that thrill of a cliff, of real danger yet rise into true greatness, and yet something to not trifle with, ever, then the process causes this person to transition through various emotional states, which include flabbergast, "ah-ah-ah," then difficult to catch a breath, puzzle, fear, hot and cold flashes, shake, very, then a trap, also known as an exception, fault or synchronous interruption, then petrify followed by thrill to no end at this great mystery, and that cycle repeats several times.

Eventually, this German patrician quickly steps back to gain safety, and further, then once at a considerable distance, out of that field or event horizon, scans the area in great detail.

Not much later, he slowly travels to the right, to a nearby door, and cautiously reaches for the doorknob then midway freezes, and waits, really waits, and something else happens, quite an unusual feeling.

So he bursts inside the room.

# CHAPTER 7

He bursts inside the room, a lumber room, a room well-heeled people have, to store custom furniture, such as built to match a theme, yet a place for things not needed now; however, they have tremendous value, so a treasure room with only one substantial way inside, and often lit by natural light, such as a narrow slot or more, although not large enough for someone to shimmy inside, and outside that slot often leads to the forbidden garden, a place other people rarely see, for any number of reasons, such as it might reveal the way and means, or serve as a sanctuary, and the best possible quiescence.

Or, it represents a work-in-progress, and an effort to restore the *apokatastasis*, a *diaspora*, such as the soul or paradise lost, or heaven on earth, yet other people might misunderstand, which seems to represent the norm of people, who see very little of any given situation yet jump to a conclusion with a heuristic, a mental shortcut, or often based on a cognitive bias.

Just as importantly, here and now, the patrician scans a few degrees at a time, left to right, as well as the ceiling then floor, yet not behind.

And he finds nothing unusual then stacks expensive furniture to precariously peer through that narrow slot, which leads to the forbidden sanctuary garden, a place other people rarely see, then a careful scan sees nothing out of the ordinary.

So he exits, and returns to that first door, the one with a tremendous mystery, and moments later, a subtle hint of pine arrives, then cedar, storax, frankincense, and Indian hemp.

However, and again, something else arrives—thistle, yes, an Asteraceae, an inflorescence star, yet as if a complex polyphyletic or thistle sage, a salvia carduacea-style system.

Then he slowly reaches for the doorknob and says "It leads everywhere, yes, everywhere," and eyes widen at the threshold, then role confusion arrives, as well as "What have I become?"

And so much so, that a reasonable person should carefully step back, far back, and especially out of each event horizon stage, out of that theater, and narrow path or window into everywhere, or flash-sideways-lost, as there also seems a considerable number of temporal fractures, as if a "drawing of the analytic extension of tetration to the complex plane," yet all hidden from sight, yet here and there, or put simply, narrow windows into these various aspects, such as flash somewhere, often in a loop, yet as if yet another television episode, at some fundamental threshold, or worst, at the very edge of existence, or out of the universe, as a reject or rejection slip, of sail on, sail away.

Then his soul shivers and eyes widen at that very edge of true greatness, the cliff, or final precipice of existence, and a thrill arrives, overwhelms, and he frequently experiences a tremendous sense of awe, which causes mouth and eyes to widen, as a person might exit the evolutionary tree, the tree of life, and become what?"

Regardless of the danger, this German patrician bursts inside that room, yet beyond that special state.

# Chapter 8

Meanwhile the boulder shifts slightly then monitors a five-year-old girl thousands of miles away; Jennifer Congrego, who greatly frustrates about something.

And she seems quite perplexed then carefully looks about then eventually plops down at her desk chair, which sits *mise en abyme*, between two mirrors, as if within an infinite reproduction of image, of infinite reality, other possibilities, frames, paths, dimensions, and infinite group theory, of group-bound dynamics, of group-think, such as same-old, same-old, yet of real possibilities.

And in complete frustration about something, she vents one loud puff of air after another, as it delays long overdue homework, which sits in a huge pile, and she wonders out loud, "Why so much homework?

"Is it a revenge thing by parents, teachers," administrators, local, state and federal government, who battle among each other for control, for dominance, or is education based on the last war, or the good old days, a vicarious memory, an elusive thing, a snippet, or education based of justification, or based on mythos, and the system adds more and more burden on a student, the system adds more snarl, more escalation?

And she might work faster, if that favorite ink pen appears; the lucky one, with a cute happy face attachment, well, to charm and delight when needed, especially during moments that frustrate, such as now.

Moments later, boulder shifts about, then against protocol, it projects a subtle beam into the room, which nudges the pen several times, and enough so, the little finally lady notices it.

And is she really a little lady, a respectable?

Meanwhile, at the mansion, Tommy boldly announces, "A Chinese food party!" then she gives a generous tip to the delivery person and passes paper plates, forks, and napkins as a huge crowd celebrates, except Mary, who sizzles then puts her head filled with regret into her hands and says, "Someone save me, take me away, there's no place like home, no place like home," as Agrippa phones an early return.

# CHAPTER 9

Elsewhere, Bonnie slips into the water, and the idea of a long soak captures her fascination, to lie there, yes, and be, to relax, exist, to drift, to find solace, and she drifts in this quiet section of the forest which offers peace as well as calm.

And as several tight beams of sunlight reaches through the dense forest canopy, which extend here and there.

And all of which gives this setting a certain poetic charm, which seems quite profound, bright, vivid, fresh, free and fair, and something a poet might enjoy or musician, or someone who needs real relief from the daily drudge, from the system, and all that chaos, much of it deliberately made so for one reason or another.

Then moments later, a light beam touches her.

In fact, it warms and provides comfort, which she notices, accepts, and moves ever so slightly to receive the full effect, especially on her face, the temple, *augurium* or tome, an executive precinct with special rules, and surrounded by an extraordinary garden, in fact, a picturesque place of colorful bloom, a virtuous treatise with function.

Then something happens, something.

Her toes uncurl then wiggle, and again.

Of equal importance, the beam soothes and helps her drift beyond time, beyond her earthly coil, where she peacefully drifts out as her consciousness unfolds and expands while basking in the warmth.

And moments later, eternity arrives, as if she lies outside and independently of time, floating in the universe, existing, in some category of being.

And that solar beam calms.

It helps guide her through eternity: that place, into that part of the universe.

Then something else happens, something.

She exists everywhere.

And moments later, the beam stops, as a cloud arrives or foliage shifts.

Regardless, the beam stops and that state-based education disappears, as if a disappearing act.

Or was it a petition, a "legal process affecting rights, obligations and duties?

And no matter what she does, that state does not return.

Yet she shifts about in search, in search of her guide into eternity, into everywhere at the same time.

Then in stages, the crude aspects of conventional time and space arrive, crude in every sense of the word as well as origin, and a crude education, a substitute, such as substitute goods and services, of second best, a dull version or an ever so dull education.

Regardless, she realizes this and still finds satisfaction, a lovely day, as it could be worse.

And all the stresses leading up to this point melt away, as toes uncurl then twinkle, and muscles relax in this spectacular tub.

So why not have, what could be a "08 - Lovely Day?"

# CHAPTER  10

By now and with a full belly, the dog sleeps nearby, yes, far enough to show respect for personal space, and it drifts down, deeper and deeper, down into the subconscious pool, down into the supercontinent, into another aspect of the canine universe.

And it might be a place where dogs rule.

And cats admire dogs.

So much so, "Ruff" is a sacred word, and only spoken by nobility, the truly noble, by a real aristocrat, especially a sovereign ruler of the empire, an imperial council as well as the supreme attestation, spoken only by those with real culture, growth, and progress, as well as genteel, refined, and well-bred, "Ruff," yes, and said with majesty, truth and beauty, "Ruff."

And "Meow" is a felony, yes, a serious crime, yet not a thought crime, as dogs are well above that, and more tolerant, a more noble specie, more civil.

And the murmur "Nnnn, nnnn, nnnn" by a puppy dog means "I love you, yes I really love you with all my heart and soul, yes I do," well, at least in that deep sleep, that world according to dogs, that supercontinent and canine universe.

However in that spectacular tub, Bonnie notices none of that, and with a held breath as well as open eyes, she submerges into the emerald water.

And Bonnie imagines being an *ama*, a Japanese skin diver in search of shellfish, *or, yes, better yet* she thinks, *do so as a mermaid, for treasure, yes, salvage a treasure, yet maybe based on Shipwrecks of the Western Hemisphere or some other classic reference book, and underwater dig in Port Royal, or Florida, or in*

*Mexican water, or at the site of a famous battle, such as with the Spanish Armada, Lepanto or some other significant, maybe the Spanish Main, yes, as a colorful mermaid, and where is The Land Baby?*

Of which, a quick breath and look above does not find, so she submerges with eyes open then explores the seven seas, and one mystery after another.

And eventually returns for a moon pie and sip of world-class booze, and during consumption she seems joyful, well, and a bit feisty, especially from the fact of surviving all that turmoil, all those trials and tribulations, all those unnatural shocks to the mind as well as soul.

"I made it to the other side.

"And this calls for a celebration, a major celebration" as toes curl and uncurl, then twinkle.

"A moon pie," which she slowly eats as well as sips ultrarare spirits, sips exceptional booze then on occasion calls for a toast, "to perseverance, to evolution and eventual graduation from that role of a red shirt."

Then she feels a bit playful, quite naughty, and why not?

So, she emerges from the tub then reveals her magnificent curves, as well as possibilities.

Then she blows gentle kisses, and lips pout, flirt as well as a wink beckons, and playfully arches her back to reveal the best curve, then another, and practices one wardrobe malfunction after another, practices various routines, such as oops, and ever so innocent then Marilyn Monroe imitations, and playfully bats eyes, flirts, tosses hair, then shows an ever so long leg, oh my.

Afterwards, in her full naked glory, she searches this collection of goods.

In fact, she shows no modesty whatsoever, and forages through one cabinet after another while considering this and that then walks about looking through one pile after another.

The entire process seems to delight her to no end, being naughty, even scandalous, "Yes," and parading about naked, proud, then now and again showing her curves, occasionally posing as a flirt, each time attempting to cast a seductive poetic spell, a spell to pull you closer and closer.

"Can you see my curves?

"Do you want to see more?"

Then she stops, finds that high-end leather suitcase, and once open, it reveals those skimpy fantasy costumes, super sexy, such as sly French maid, demanding pirate, incorruptible cop, sailor on leave, perky head cheerleader, innocent Miss Bunny, then an all-powerful CEO, and rich beyond description.

Then another outfit intrigues her, a wild cowgirl with whip, a bullwhip, which she cracks again and again, "Yes," as her eyes light.

However, as all that high-octane booze gains influence, serious influence, and grogginess arrives, very much so then standing seems quite impractical.

And eventually she feels the need to sleep then returns to that small wooden bed, which might remind a person of a *Forrest Bed, The Architect's Brother*, yet one that contains *peony* shrubs and something else, which she tests for comfort, and "Yes, that's nice, very, and the way it should have been all along, and in the beginning."

Then groggy thoughts arrive, of a golden age, the classical and Renaissance, Renaissance Humanism, Neoclassicism and the Age of Enlightenment, and the Romantic era version, the original long-lost glory now found.

Moreover, the process does so as if a liminal master of ceremony, the phase transition, and done as if a noble experiment, which honors the classics, and yet as a bold new frontier of a threshold adventure.

So she smiles then sleeps.

Yet something else happens, something.

She receives a feeling, of sinking, of trouble, her trouble tree, and each branch seems ever so clear.

So much so, she quickly wakes then realizes a gained specie arrives next to her, yes, a cloaked thing, which closely studies her mind, and inside personal space, and similar to what happened to the Punk Buster, the Freak, and the type of things that often happen in free enterprise, especially in this type of forest or near that forest old-growth tree.

And that gained specie conducts a few secret experiments on her, such as a variation of *Star Trek: Voyager, Scientific Method*, in search of something.

Yet she pretends to not notice, and stay especially calm.

Regardless, the dog notices, which seems to irritate that cloaked thing to no end, in fact seriously irritates, as if the dog has no right to disturb progress, real progress, especially of a superior being, someone above the law, an exigent circumstance, with emergency powers or a sovereign, such as "I can change the rules at any time or place," or gerrymander at will, and declare a landslide, a mandate, and never look directly at me, well, because you are beneath me, quite, not even remotely close, that system of thought, that history of authority.

And enough so, that cloaked thing concerns, yet the dog refuses to break eye contact, and is not impressed then the specie departs deep into the ultradense forest, which the dog follows.

Immediately, Bonnie notices, as well as the serious canine intent, and follows the dog through dense forest over a considerable distance.

Eventually she arrives just in time, as something snatches the dog underground, just like that, gone.

Of which, it bothers her to no end.

Well, not because she loves the dog, or likes it; because the dog truly annoys her, and since the very beginning of this ill-fated property markers mission.

It bothers her because no one should be treated that way, period.

So she dives into that deep hole, and through a considerable amount of dirt, dust and rumble, which eventually leads through one complex passage after another then door.

Well, something happens once there.

She snaps, mentally, goes insane, maybe clinically insane, or the new age equivalent, and from a lifetime of slights, from the thought of being pushed around once too often, run off one too many times, bullied through her life for being different, picked on again, and again, which may trigger genes, stubborn genes, or it could have been from that last tremendous impact, or from something else such as fate, luck, or the randomness of nature, maybe from the thrownness of nature.

Regardless, the mechanism delivers waves of fuel and gameness, as in a powerful and raw tenacious spirit, an indestructible aspect of the human spirit.

Moreover, Bonnie takes it personal, very, and seems wholly offended down to the core, the marrow, the *hortus conclusus*, as well as incorporeal and liminal coil.

And she seems far less concerned about risk, and more about the bedrock principle, of being treated as "a mere ragdoll, banged about, rudely dragged here and there through one punishing menace after another, then summarily slung from the forest a few times," as well as for all those previous slights received over a lifetime, all those pernicious pecks, and especially all those lost opportunities.

Then an impulse urges her to kick down that door.

Moments later, eyes narrow.

Moreover, the jaw muscles repeatedly tense then teeth grind, really grind, and to convey readiness, resolve and grit—true grit.

Stubbornness does run in her family, especially her mother.

However, Bonnie had been the exception, a person easily wounded, and more than willing to retreat from confrontation, or surrender then go along with the situation, to maintain the peace, yet each time and underneath it all, these feeling went unresolved then eventually pestered the mind, and often.

Where, they become stuck in a loop, and similar to how an image, phrase or song becomes stuck in the mind for one reason or another, and what is that process, as if stuck in a temporal loop, or stuck in a certain segment of time as well as space?

She snaps, kicks down the door then super kicks that creature, just like: pow! and lights out so to speak, and that thing or creature falls like a mighty oak tree, then she super kicks another creature that emerges from behind the curtain.

And apparently they were ultimately behind that end of days, eschatology, the final events of history, the ultimate human destiny, end of time, and ultimate fate of the universe.

They secretly fed fuel, kept the turmoil going, as it would have extinguished long ago, as the universe has a self-correcting ability, a localized function to prevent a warp bubble pierce, a puncture of the universal spacetime fabric then collapse the supreme algebraic bubble, the supreme bulkhead or bulkheads, the quintessential stack, such as how to remove all that space in-between everything, and do so faster than the speed of light, for example the harmonics and overtones of deflation, as well as spacetime dependency on symmetrics for an expansion, for example the bell-shaped curve distribution.

That happens, things like that happen all the time, the meek have had enough, such as enough is enough, and pow!

It goes to show you, never underestimate a woman, or man, child or parent, especially a mother, or any human, whether black, white or whatever, or redneck, Appalachian, American Indian, or any form of Indian, never underestimate a native or immigrant, or whomever, never underestimate anyone, ever. And just as importantly be reasonable, thoughtful, polite and show respect, or somehow, someway, and maybe not today, maybe not for 10,000 years, yet someday when you least suspect it, such as when you feel so superior, so righteous and pure, and the feud dynamics of escalation, or the petty, pettifog of conflict, or worse yet, pleasure from pain, pleasure from others that suffer, that crisscross, and cackle at severe damage, or just as significantly show indifference, especially to collateral damage, and the suffering of others, or no idea why others fuss about it, so, never underestimate someone, nature or the universe?

Or you could say it another way, such as "Kicks ass and takes names," or "Chew bubblegum and kick ass."

And it happened so fast, no thought whatsoever, especially about the danger or full consequences, as she was supposed to be meek, at least from all the reports.

So these things or creatures revive then flee into an event, into what a person might say resembles a "tetration analytic extension," a complex function as per Dmitrii Kouznetosv, or analytic extension of the Ackermann function, an exceptionally complex route then quickly out of the universe, just like that, gone.

Of which Bonnie leaps inside that event to follow, yet once inside experiences tremendous forces, complex patterns, options, most red herrings, isolated bits, space, time, places to follow or leap to, as if steps or ever so small islands, many paths loop, some paths travel as if a wave, some nearly as if a circle yet end as what, and some push sideways in time and/or space?

Just as importantly, all seem correct in their own right once there, yet most seem incorrect in relationship to each other.

However, to a conventional mindset or perspective, it seems bizarre, quite, and lack logic, such as inductive, abductive, and deductive.

It defies common sense and seems absurdly dangerous.

So much so, it floods the body with so many different emotions, one after another, and too many to list, such as squeamish to lip trembles, serious regret, warm tears flow, true pathos arrives in a sinister place beyond description then a brief joy as odd as that seems, and awe at a truly great mystery, and that cycle continues of mostly true pathos then brief joy, which in very distinct stages eventually exhausts the mind, body and soul.

Then a full realization arrives, you not in the same league, and not remotely qualified, ever.

As this event seems beyond rhyme or reason, and she often strays from the "mythology of lost," because there appears no decent direct route through this complex estate, just ever so strange options, such as sideways through time, and so many weird choices, and no decent route in every sense of the word.

Then once well inside, she becomes trapped, panics, and then tries to retrace steps out in a desperate struggle.

However, she seems lost beyond reason, and apparently forever with no way out, as lips quiver then other feelings arrive of serious regret, warm tears, true pathos beyond description in this sinister place.

# CHAPTER

O nce out of that complex event, and completely exhausted, she pledges to "never try that again, such as find a calendar, no something permanent, yes, for example: chisel it into an enormous block of granite, yes, chip at the stone, at various angles; yes, chisel a message, a warning."

And with the dog under an arm, she stumbles down one bunker passage way after another then through that door, climbs the hole, emerges from the hidden entrance then staggers to that safe zone with moon pies, bathtub, bed and especially booze, to recover.

And with a stiff drink, the world's most expensive booze, and another and another, she passes out on that bed.

# CHAPTER

In the meantime, elsewhere within the underground bunker system and carefully handling extremely hazardous waste, the Punk Buster notices something, the material gradually loses power and toxicity for some unknown reason, and time seems more normal, the local timeline: the flow.

All of which greatly speeds the cleaning process as well as repair of more underground bunker systems, which maintain forest shadows, snares, pits and other wiles, as well as repair of more worldwide abilities to deliver retribution against trespassers.

However these efforts do nothing to repair the future, repair the throne, the official residence and fortified crown that has a human aspect, yet of supreme technocracy and unquestionable glory.

And soon it will have time to chase those things along that passageway, and of equal importance, it needs to resolve that other mystery, those cloaked gained species, which often conduct secret experiments, especially on it, and surprisingly those species are now nowhere in sight. And of equal importance, it needs to decipher that cloaking system, the process, just in case they return. So it can have a known advantage, and maybe trap them then conduct a few tests, considerable ones, to reveal their biology as well as technology, to explore their abilities and limits; as all systems have limits, and they often run off a Zen survivor, visionary, truth-telling sage, good shepherd, or wasteland elder.

# CHAPTER 13

Elsewhere, Cub recovers from that sudden abandon ship-abandon ship!

As she startled, and had to quickly abandon that backpack then struggle to a safe distance.

Normally, Cub, her name represents a short version of Somni Cub-Cullera, yet everyone called her Cub, wears this elaborate backpack computer everywhere, well, almost everywhere, not swimming, however it is waterproof, full submersible, and at night it hangs on the wall, to recharge, regardless of the solar component, and the pack hangs in niche, sweet spot, nexus, yet portico, third space, which also has an aedicula aspect, for ceremonial images, substance, and rare incense, and yet the primary function is a conversation pit, or as if a well of souls, though something else, something beyond words, beyond all language.

It sits there at night, to recharge, well, a best-effort charge, as a full charge seems rare indeed, quite, as some things rarely restore to original intent or condition, the original mission, such as part of the universal garden, where maybe ninety-nine percent of all species to ever live on Earth are extinct, are lost solutions to a very complex system, puzzle as well as the dilemma, and that any given action can have profound implications, such as step on an ant, and really mash it, or step on a species for whatever reason, as compared to a person or community need for another strip mall, another common place, or common-reuse principle, common-gate or common admission test: that profound lost dilemma, which at the time often seems minor to many people, especially powers-that-be, The Boss man, Mr. Big or Ms. Big or large-and-in-charge or too-big-to-fail, so just keep your head down and keep digging.

This woman has some traits of artist Nathalie Mieback, as well as a poet, math forecast specialist, and someone who understands resonance-phenomenon-natural frequency, collectively exhaustive events, oneiromancy outlier events, open source higher-order functions, and has advanced zombie survival guide skills.

Which, the latter does not refer to the classic voodoo or cult zombie, but how any given system might train members into meekness, and/or to be a follower, with no executive thinking skills, or an ever so shallow version. Well, and she also organizes "zombie walks, pub crawls" for charitable and political causes, to raise awareness about zombie rights in a soulless ancient and modern systems, of the Big Show. As people are often treated as if mere stagecraft, theatrical scenery, theatrical property, or a principal with the least privilege and relegated a role, an ever so flat script. For instance, defend an idea, belief system or powers-that-be with that shallow language game; that chase, or defend a virtue, or an internal meek, such as bacteria, virus, viroid or metazoa, or some combination, which steers the agenda and defend as fandom with all those traits of same-old, same-old, the history of civilization, of ideas, life, yet often as a trope, in an common quagmire?

And Cub often plays a mandolin in the David Grisman folk style or performs as an *Occitan* troubadour, to a very select set of exclusive clients, and often sings a solution created by very complex algorithms, from that elaborate basket backpack computer, which contains colorful lights as well as posts, wires, detailed notes, embedded messages, insertions, and strings.

And normally with the backpack, Cub tracks maneuvering among very powerful special interests, such as the cruel, unusual and hyper, especially interests that promote "all or nothing, my way or else," and doomsday, end time, end of days, or some other cultural equivalent, such as during an election, promotion, quarterly profit squeeze or other timeline, that process and industry of. And they have the abilities to create the feelings of, which often mean not necessarily a true End of

Days, eschatology, yet they often have some substancial ability, such as a local, regional, or nation-state basis.

However, more importantly, as well here and now, the backpack continues to make a considerable amount of noise and shudders then quite a disturbing cycle of clamor, of crisis, and one profound presaging event after another then it seems as if an exceptional thing, as well as a *sui generis* then almost human, not a normal human, a regular Joe or Jane, but a transhuman might emerge, well, if need be, if circumstances require a special something.

So, she does what any respectable person would do: she pokes it, and not a mean poke, not rude, or as a complaint, but gentle, to see if it needs something, something special, maybe vital.

And it does not then settles down, as if a sunken kingdom, or the female version, as if a metaphysical poet, such as a T S Elliot product.

Then it scans the surrounding space, as well as time, for a rollback event, and who could issue a major rollback of the universe, such as a true steward or trustee, an exceptional plenipotentiary, or special stateless elite, or extraordinary Davos person with a prerogative, an exclusive right to move toward the exit.

Not much later, it returns to the original state, a backpack computer as well as ever so peaceful, with an occasional blinking light here and there, as if a peaceful world unto itself, and not something else, SOS, abandon ship, abandon ship!

# CHAPTER 14

Elsewhere and over the next few weekends, Agrippa carefully investigates the mystery man, his identity, and each new lead, each branch, well, because fingerprints reveal nothing, nor dental records, as the comatose man has the maximum number of teeth, which have a certain appearance; in fact, quite nice as all seem remarkably fit, well-maintained, and have a superb symmetry, OK-OK perfect teeth if such exist, perfect pearly whites, or said another way textbook, ideal, with just the right size, shape, zero filling and no chips, wear marks, caps, crowns, bridges; none, perfect, and just the right color.

So, she focuses on that complex diving suit, which contains a wealth of parts, devices, compartments, and hidden functions.

As nearly all aspects appear custom-made, including the valves, anchor bolts, captive fasteners, Clekos, retaining rings, as well as gaskets, screws, sprockets, specialty bearings, compression coil, air manifold, and heating coil.

The system also contains commutators, reservoir tanks, hidden hoisting rings, mooring clamps, a carbon dioxide scrubber, as well as what appears as if an emergency panic control system for claustrophobia, which releases a gas, a complex sedative, yet as an atonement, at least according to Mary. And it "bends the mind," to "improve abstract thought, especially the executive function," and "a process that alters neurochemicals, such as neurotransmitters, enzymes and hormones."

Plus more technical terms, quite, however during the conversation, Agrippa drifts elsewhere in the universe as well as her memory, through her troubled tree, which often happens to a person, place or thing, especially a system, it drifts far way yet within for whatever reason, such as a lack of essentials, and needed at just the right moment during each significant growth moment yet fed fluff, artificial whatnot sold as vital, or whatever the bandwagon offers.

Just as significantly, each effort to discreetly resolve all of these suit aspects, open more questions about its properties, the mechanical, electrical, thermal, chemical, magnetic, as well as optical, acoustical, radiological and biological support systems.

And before each trip, she asks Mary to babysit that comatose man, the unconscious red-haired man who resembles a Thracian, a freed man, a peltast, such as an Agrianian peltast.

And each time Mary flinches, grumbles about this and that, which Agrippa does not see, hear, understand or accept, or she chooses to conveniently ignore.

Yet in the end, Mary always agrees by default, maybe by not protesting loud enough or the right way, which represents life, or better yet, a history of the human species, especially in "so-called civilizations," as much of burden sits on the protestor, OK-OK, to weigh down, such as a waddle here and there, especially in during competition.

And after a system collapses people often charge, "You didn't speak up!" and a charge often made by a people or system that acts as if born yesterday, or seems relatively new and does truly understand human history, or they have an exceptionally poor memory, or an inability to develop complex thought, especially about human nature, top-down systems, authoritarianism, totalitarian, even stratocracy, and the current crop of ever so shallow democracies with gerrymandered channels, as well as the concentration of power, stubbornness and obsession.

All of which puts enormous pressure on Mary, who already has a considerable number of problems, especially at work, as well as her efforts to earn an advance nursing degree, that seven-day grind, and from the bias against a nursing doctorate program. As no one explained to her in advance about prejudice against the nursing field, the systemic aspect, the institutional bias, where many medical doctors show open contempt and prejudice against nurses, especially those who earn a doctorate in nursing practice.

And the mere mention of someone calling a nurse "doctor" causes many medical doctors to cringe, knot, feel a slight then show open contempt, such as a primitive reflex to peck, bully and wound, as well as set the "record straight," and some of them take pleasure in subterfuge, as a trickster who deploys cruel and unusual methods, as a lesson.

Yet if discovered, they might call it "tough love" or some other euphemism, or immediately launch into loaded language, loaded terms or emotive language then deliberately incite a classic ballroom blitz, "Become the man at the back who said, everyone attack! And it turned into a ballroom blitz, and the girl in the corner said, Boy, I wanna warn ya, it'll turn into a ballroom blitz."

Of which, it seems a reoccurring theme throughout human history, regardless of profession or system, a classic version of so-called love, such as love me completely or else, or a love and devotion that often travels one way, and is often seen in many other social constructs, which include gender, family, friend, tribe, team, employer, town, politic, culture, religion, race, and much more.

As a result, all these pecks have taken their toll on Mary, on her point of view, as well as demeanor and self-worth.

Life has ground things out of her, ground charm out, as well as perk, and she says now and again, "Time spent babysitting time could be used elsewhere, such as a major reorganization of clutter, and sleep—yes, a peaceful sleep, maybe in a comfy chair, oh yes, in the mansion backyard garden among aromatic beds of peppermint, lemon balm, lavender and fennel in bloom, in that Elizabethan Indigo-colored lounge chair, which has the full appearance of world-class comfort.

"The kind you sit in, sink down and say in an extended way, Ah, now that's the way it should be—life, yes."

Then said ever so slowly as if contemplating a slow universal wave function, "Yes," she could sit outside the mansion, which has many similarities to The Breakers, a Vanderbilt mansion with terra-cotta red roof tiles and Indiana limestone walls.

However, this Gilded Age home has only twenty-two rooms and consumes 18,000 square feet.

And the landscape contains large weeping willows, majestic oaks and mature red maples, as well as plants in bloom, which include a wide variety of rhododendrons, laurels, and dogwoods.

In addition, all add to the overall charm, and give the place a certain poetic beauty, especially from the symmetry of design, foliage, and vivid colors.

It gives the place a certain image of prosperity, progress and peace, a place in full accord with nature, as if it represents an unofficial paradise, a deep foundation, one of the finest examples of earthfast, a substancial post, and what a person might expect within the golden age of the classical and Renaissance gardens, a place that might lead into the transcendent, might trigger a full restoration of glory, the original long-lost glory now found.

Mary had often noticed, briefly scanned, and seriously considered the charm which activated a full imagination, especially from an adventurous footpath that leads to one not-so-secret garden after another, a trial garden, and each garden with a microclimate, as well as stylistic allure, with full potential, spacious, grand, and noble.

Others sit in small niches, such as inside a small bamboo grove, or under the full protection of a weeping willow in bloom, or between huge ceremonial boulder crops, for example an ancient rock culture, a prehistoric tribute, which form a poetic megalithic boulder garden shrine that enables rare and sacred space to form, and in anyone of these places, a person might sit, meditate, and ponder the great mysteries of the universe, as an explorer, third culture person, psychonautic, transformative, grok or kythe agent, or equilibrium refinement.

Many of those picturesque gardens have their own unique style and colorful flowers in full bloom, as well as shrubs and subshrubs, along with distinct thematic herbal sections, which sit on spectacular elevated beds that convey specific stages and nuisances within secular as well as sacred space, such as philosophical and therapeutic nuisances that cultivate, redeem, regenerate, transform, evolve and expand, as in a place pristine, vivid, free and fair, a place wholly natural and absolutely fascinating, a place for artists, poets, scholars, and even a place for romance, yes, such as romance of Palamedes, or science.

# CHAPTER 15

And of equal importance, Mary continues to secretly delegate babysitting to Emma, Mel, as well as Benny.

And once Agrippa leaves for the weekend, and with a precise pattern, Friday evening, then one or more of these substitutes quickly arrive to replace Mary, then Mary eventually returns Sunday morning well before Agrippa arrives late Sunday evening, which represents more than enough time to insure all is well.

However, as well as slowly but surely, Mary returns later and later, and on occasions, in the nick of time, with minutes to spare.

And of note, Mary does not realize her surrogates often delegate responsibility during those days, and to people not on the approved list, especially when Mary fails to bring along that adorable niece, which was their main motive, a love of her, such as, how often does a person find true love, as opposed to settle for close enough, and someone with bad habits?

In addition, all their obvious and subtle hints to Mary as well as one another about that subject do not register, which might represent another example of human history, a fair as well as reasonable notice, a reasonable, practical and important request, a major adjustment, yet no significant change to the system, and if so then a cosmetic adjustment, or add another layer, such as snarl or entanglement, as Mary seems more and more preoccupied with her rut, the world according to that rut.

Just as significantly and each time, the new secret delegation chain grows more complex, and as the weeks go by this circle widens to include Reece, Vera and even Samantha, then eventually expands even further without Mary's knowledge, to include Zoey, Cub and Tommy, as well as their friends, and Vay, the quintessential "It Girl," one of those persons who can go by one name, which represents a curious phenomenon.

How can a person gain worldwide recognition and do so with a single name?

What traits have universal appeal?

What type of person can slowly move through the crowd and that causes social eddies to neatly pull people to and fro, as if a hidden misaligned gradient pressure, such as the baroclinic instability, for lack of a better phrase?

Just as importantly, this woman seems to be everyone's first choice.

However, Vay resembles the unattainable, the one people want to be near yet cannot have, which may represent a function of nature, such as the physis?

Just as importantly, much of life seems that way—where people must settle for a very pale substitute, for ideas, persons, places or things far down the ladder—and dozens of steps or more, and quite far from their first choice, from natural aspiration, especially vital needs, vital requirements—and people must settle for things not quite compatible, often artificial, such as the golden age of plastic, which seems everywhere, especially in the body.

And if you really think about it, really, you can taste plastic and feel it, feel the influence on thoughts, on the reference threshold, and influence on emotion, mood, temperament, personality, disposition, and motivation, that type of complex interdependency of mental systems, yes, taste the plastic, which the nation-state systems embed in as many products, places and services as possible, that obsession.

And does it pollute the mind, body and soul?

And will it have a profound effect on the human evolutionary timeline, such as a shortcut, maybe a highway to hell, that rush, and escalation, which seems quite apparent according to news broadcast, who often proclaim the end of days, *Four Horsemen of the Apocalypse,* the last few days, final days, eschaton, end of time, of history, the ultimate destiny of the human species as well as the universe, with fire, brimstone, tremendous suffering then supreme rollback.

Or maybe plastic, piles of it will lead to heaven, maybe, or a sideway venture, into yet another bizarre cultural venture, another social construct, a tool if you will, or bazaar, which might represent confusion for a considerable amount of time, for decades or centuries, from unintended consequences, from a need to adjust, well, because the body took billions of years to gain this coalition, the biome, and might need more time for the new norm, the new culture, which the microbiome eventually gains an equilibrium?

However a bible thumper might say humans began "10,000 years ago, or so."

And back to the point of settling for less than ideal, as people must often settle for a substitute, for a pale substitute, for one nonessential after another, and for things that do not quite fit or fully square, and strangely enough often mandated by law, by the system, the caretaker, institution or too-big-to-fail, or by the large-and-in-charge, or Mr. Big or Miss Big, or the man or woman behind the man, or the ultimate authority, the da chief, or the load-bearing boss, or champion planar.

They mandate a poor fit.

This mandate, or so many mandates, too many to count might defy universal law, physics, and the classics of a stable configuration, such as how to properly sit, as well as travel in high-dimensional topology, in spacetime, and discreetly, as a best-effort grok or anchor in the great spectacular, in the big ugly.

And they say it must fit, the law says so, the system, boss, parents, friends, neighbors, race, gender, economic system, and so on, and often they are the great pretender, a fake, a phony, a false prophet, or some combination of. Or more likely they fail to realize the implications of that initial decision, the foundation, a Hobbesian trap, especially binary thought that leads to fear and mutual distrust between actors as well as a preemptive strike. And does this add to world turmoil, to the confusion, agitation, commotion of life, and add another layer of snarl, such as to the great string, as if the universe might represent a single string, a tangled strain of Christmas lights or whatever, a whatnot, whatchamacallit, or thingamajig mostly hidden?

Or said another way, and in the military industrial complex, or iron triangle terms with the acronym VUCA, does that phenomenon add to the volatility, uncertainty, complexity, and ambiguity, add to misunderstanding or poor communication, or result in the abnormal need for speed, to rush, for heuristics, for one shortcut after another, that obsession or need for sugar and starch, for a sound bite, or for something that must fit on a bumper sticker?

Regardless and long sought after, social circles want Vay, and she babysits on occasion, which draws a considerable crowd, especially aristocrats, socialites, fashion icons, hedge fund managers, venture capitalists, elite bankers, political power brokers, and other groups such as fashionistas and hauterflies, who often huddle that at a distance and take great pride in well-crafted nips, pecks, and blunt critiques—as everyone and everything appears fair game to this criticism formulated to wither targets.

So much so these critics scan and study guest from head to toe, as well as the setting, then impulse comments, and criticize best friends, who moments ago, received their heartfelt welcome, warm hug, unconditional joy, intimate eye contact, and over-the-top praise, yet have moved on and mingle elsewhere.

However, and eventually, these fashionistas and hauterflies grow quite bold, especially in numbers, which maybe a universal phenomenon, a bubble, or the addictive power of a herd, a swarm at the tipping point, or the virtuous and vicious circle, and these people seem unable or unwilling to manage the volume of their voices, which gradually changes from *pianississimo*, or extremely soft, to *fortissimo*, very loud, which only adds to the event tipping point—as they say whatever the mind sparks, such as a free association, and a considerable amount seems quite insightful, however a significant amount seem ever so cruel and personal.

Eventually, this process gives the full appearance of bullies, yet not common thugs, not kinetic, with brute force or step on an ant and really mash it.

However, it resembles people who impulse, filter less, have overly sensitive thin skin, and for some seem as if a self-absorbed prickly me, an easily tippable being, such as a minor event would tip their mood, and that new mood would last much of day, as if biological products coursed through the body, and took that long to settle into less susceptible regions.

Just as importantly, as well as here and now, many of the these fashionistas and hauterflies sly impulse to intimidate others with a peck, as well as the art of deliberately planting things, such as planting rot or gossip, to make something barren, which maybe the thing these speakers fear the most, that form of attack by others.

So they attack first, a first strike, as well as that cycle of escalation, misunderstanding and turmoil then puzzle about the petty other, and why they have such thin skin, and why the self is so vulnerable, so raw. And they need to create an answer, a timeless solution, something fashion forward, and yet true classic that protects the self, protects the soul with a certain honor and glory, as if armor?

This style shares a few traits with a common and well-educated thug. Both of them specialize in tormenting the opposition, especially the weak; both use impulse, inflation, overbear, bluster, and grow bold in numbers.

Regardless of all that and regarding Vay, even women stir and lose their script in her presence, and they gush—really gush.

However, most people soon realize the near impossibility— and one at a time, a few of them approach Vay, even an aristocrat, socialite, fashion icon and each time a person walks towards her, and yet they end up elsewhere, from a series of subconscious mental constructs, which triggers along the way, and formulates a complex solution without the normal level of awareness—the iceberg phenomenon—so much so the bulk of consciousness and formulation remains hidden. And more importantly, the solution deflects that person several degrees to a new path, which eventually arcs around her.

Worse yet, a person might arrive face-to-face then self-arrest with a mysterious state of mutter, babble, or ramble on and on, about this or that in a trivial pursuit. Or, they awkwardly use one very tired cliché after another, or become stuck in a series of gush. Or, worse yet, they become stuck in an exceptionally goofy mindset, and all that embarrassment might last a lifetime, even a few generations, where that person's name might become a cautionary verb, a warning told especially to wide-eyed toddlers, kids, and young adults who stray from a straight and narrow path.

Regardless, Vay as well as other babysitters use an elaborate switch technique during the weekends, and Mary seems quite oblivious, worn out and exhausted.

However and during one of her usual slogs to the mansion on Sunday, where each leg lift seems ever so heavy, she jolts to find Quinn as a babysitter.

And Quinn eagerly greets her, seems ever so happy to help and says, "I'm here, everything is okay," pats the air then explains a remarkable list of care accomplishments, and she made dinner, which also seems, well, noteworthy, and what a person might associate with true excellence as a chef, a *chef de cuisine*, or *sauté* chef.

Yet Mary carefully studies her head-to-toe a few times then says, "I have absolutely no idea who you are."

"I'm Quinn, remember?

"We met at the mansion fundraiser, and few others times," then she continues to eagerly talk-and-talk, in fact, gushes and seems ever so satisfied, and does so as a well-being indeed, with a remarkable glow, the type people most often seek, and would trade a great fortune for, would trade all they own right then and there, yet Mary notices none of that.

For some reason—maybe it was the workload, tone, rhythm, topic, time of day, day of the week, cycle of the moon, or position of the earth as it circles around the sun, or position of the sun as it travels through space along with other solar interstellar neighbors in the Milky Way Galaxy, local galactic group, Virgo supercluster, local superclusters in the observable universe, or with relationship to other universes, multiverses, in the supreme algebraic stack or bulkhead, or it may be a minor aspect, such as low blood sugar.

However, Mary hears "blah-blah-blah" and glazes over, and mentally drifts elsewhere, and into a place where the brain does not properly translate sound, or transmutation, or translational drift, where a person drifts away as if through space-time yet within.

And for five minutes this woman, this well-being on the rise, with a remarkable glow joyfully goes on and on with happiness to finally "be a part of their lives, to be accepted and included."

Eventually Mary says, "Okay, but I still have absolutely no idea who you are.

"And I don't remember any of that," which causes a spark in Quinn, who slowly fades, slowly loses value, substance, and eventually become quite common, such as a common tone, a commonplace.

Which often happens in life, to people, places and things, to family, tribe, team, political party, institution, religion, nation, gender, race and other constructs, such as other economic systems, to other systems of thought; quickly marginalized, as gains devalued, and rare opportunities often lost, and they will not fully restore once gone.

And off to the side in a comprehensive stealth, outside a window, the creature boulder smolders as well as duly notes: "Another lost opportunity—gone, another paradise lost."

# CHAPTER

In the meantime, Agrippa continues the investigation, and departs late Friday then returns late Sunday night, and each time tries to maximize available time to follow each and every clues, as well as gather the maximum information while trying to maintain an ever so low profile, to avoid suspicion.

And her desk planner shows a meticulous schedule of people, companies, subjects, phone numbers and places, such as Huntington Beach, Wichita, Kansas City, Broken Arrow, Huntsville, Van Nuys, Columbus, Kingsville, Bloomington, and Pompano Beach.

And before each trip, Mary arrives at the mansion to babysit then departs once her replacement arrives, and normally within an hour or so.

However this delegation process grows more complex, as more people enter the mix, and they invite their friends after she departs.

So much so word spreads yet Mary seems unaware of most activity, well because people meticulously clean with a special system, an elaborate effort, then exit before she returns, and they do so in a well-organized secretive fashion, as discreet as possible.

And of equal importance secret upscale socials form, gatherings, yet eventually evolve into parties, and each party has its own uniqueness, such as a theme party, which become the rage and they include a genuine western hoedown, rave, role-playing, recreated high school dance, and scary genre.

The events on occasion include surprise, whodunit, hillbilly hoedowns, pirates and wenches, pagan spoof, cuddle, and slumber.

Then on other occasions it includes classic antiquity, such as major Greco-Roman events, Greco-Roman mystery cults of Attis, Cybele, and Trophonius, as well as mysteries of Dionysian, Eleusinian, Mithraic, and Orphic, as well as Villa of the Mysteries.

And on more than a few occasions the mansion features 1950's cocktail, high tea, princess for a day, and elite fund-raising.

Then at last the minute, Tommy cancels a foam party, where a machine ejects a tremendous amounts of foam, well because she thought it over the top and too risky, especially the cleanup, and "How does the cleaning process work?

"How do you remove rooms full of foam nearly five feet deep?"

Just as significantly and over all, these events grow more and more elaborate, such as live bands, and worldclass names, then exotic themes become the norm.

In fact, the buzz travels a great distance, to far parts of the country, along with a very strict timetable, rules and who might attend, which develops into an ever so exclusive list.

And each time, the event shuts down well ahead of schedule, well before early Sunday morning, which allows more than enough time to clean, restore, and move traffic.

Of equal importance, most people work as a team, to put everything back in place, and they seem quite civil, remarkable in fact, and they rely on a detailed set of before-photographs mounted in an ever so thick three-ring binder, to insure everything returns to the exact place.

So, hours before Mary arrives on Sunday late morning, things have already fully restored, plus everyone has departed except the designated babysitter, who patiently wait with a beaming smile, as a full spectrum of course, according to the theory, yet done in a way that does not raise concerns, does not seem too happy as well as too satisfied, well, because most people rarely achieve that in a given day, a full spectrum, such as elated and enthusiastic, that mode of discover, which represents something a person might experience in a gold rush, of someone who has found a truly great fortune, a California dream or some other version, such as the Klondike, Australia, New Zealand, South Africa, South America, for example the Brazilian gold rush and Tierra del Fuego, that look.

# CHAPTER

Today, Agrippa makes final preparations for another trip, and stuffs a small suitcase with the bare minimum, a single clothing change and a few other items then she carefully examines the desk Day-Timer for contact details, as Mary looks on.

And within three hours, she boards an airplane to Seattle, Washington, which Mary verifies by cell phone then arranges a substitute, someone to care for the comatose man.

However, no one seems willing to step forward and volunteer, no one.

In fact, call after call finds an excuse, and each excuse has an over-the-top aspect, as well as ever so complex, which seems far-fetched, colorful, and quite vivid.

And each conversation starts well enough, normal, with small talk, yet the moment she asks for babysitting help, a long pause arrives, then an over-the-top story begins, a long story, and one that contains an enormous amount of detail which lack logic, and that person talks and talks, the nervous type, such as *If I could only stop talking … please stop talking,* that lack of self-control.

In addition, this spontaneous story gains a certain momentum, an escalation, a life of its own, which happens to people as well as systems more often than not, a founding *mythos,* a figure of speech scheme, as the process seems easy to start, such as something based on an idea or principle, and yet it becomes exceptionally difficult to resolve, and do so neatly, for example with an ever so soft landing in sight, or insight, and with few unintended consequences, ripples or impact!

Of equal importance, Mary does not know, most of these friends gather at Samantha's house and listen to each conversation in fear, fear that things will unravel, as each party quickly gains a life of its own, word spreads fast, so much so uninvited guests arrive, and often powerful interests, too-big-to-fail.

So after the last phone call, they reach an agreement to avoid the mansion this weekend, with no dissenting votes, none, no grumbles, no holdouts, no "Wait-a-minute, can we talk about it in great detail?" And they show no hint of disagreement, no subtle body language that shows a reservation, no poker tells or masked feelings, such as a hidden stub or sunken empire to reemerge.

In fact, they raise the right hand then solemnly pledge a loyalty oath, and "I further swear."

And all the while, they carefully look at each other, especially the eyes for an oath-breaker, for someone who might betray the great sisterhood, betray the trust of "so help me," as if the Oath of Strasbourg.

Again, everyone agreed to stay away from the mansion.

Then heads nod in full agreement.

Elsewhere, Mary needs a babysitter option, scans her phone directory then digs through papers, through piles of this and that.

She finds nothing, well, except serious concern, frustration, and grumble then says things unfit for print, things a real lady would not say.

Desperate, she enters her car, and digs in long forgotten piles of stuff, and neglected for one reason or another, in boxes filled with stuff, with things never quite gotten to, clipped articles, napkin notes, magazines, late bills, receipts, novels, how to organize books, as well as one to-do-list after another, stuff received by mail yet not opened, scribbled ideas on irregular slips of paper, a lost button now found, plus and an odd sock.

Then she grumbles more things unfit for print, and the head bobs with each emphatic point, well, until a point-of-no-return.

Finally, she locates a phone number napkin with no name, just a phone number.

So, what would you do?

Mary calls.

And after four rings, a woman answers, which Mary does not recognize, yet bides for more time with an over-the-top greeting, one given to a long-lost friend you finally meet again, or to a perfect stranger, that technique to quickly remove a substantial barrier, and create a proper mood or considerable inclusiveness, the best possible type.

Of equal importance, she uses small talk, the art of, in fact a clinic on how to, and uses a series of cold-read conversation starters about the weather and current events, as if at the office and just another day or out for a walk, to stretch the legs then ask a favor, that technique.

And to her shock, the woman agrees, a woman she still does not remember, does not know the name, yet has a phone number, and the bluff works.

So much so, and within two hours, someone knocks on the massive mansion doors, which causes Mary to startle, well, because people rarely use that entrance, except a Jehovah's Witness, a millenarian restorationist, a person seriously concerned about destruction of the present world system, about an approaching Armageddon, which includes a gathering of armies for an end–times battle.

Then Mary remembers the last episode, the last Jehovah's Witness mansion visit, when they immediately offered words of wisdom then said in unison, "Trouble is part of your life, and if you don't share it, you don't give the person who loves you a chance to love you enough."

And at that time, Mary seriously considered then her head tilted a few times, looked about then said, "That's Dinah Shore."

They continued, "We're growing a strange crop of agnostics this year."

"That's E. K. Hornbeck."

"Then why did God plague us with the capacity to think?

"Mr. Brady, why do you deny the one thing that sets us above the other animals?

"What other merit have we?

"The elephant is larger, the horse stronger and swifter, the butterfly more beautiful, the mosquito more prolific, even the sponge is more durable.

Or does a sponge think?"

"Henry Drummond?"

And they continued, "Fanaticism and ignorance is forever busy and needs feeding."

"Jerome Lawrence?"

They continued, "A gem cannot be polished without friction, nor a man perfected without trials."

She puzzled, flinched, looked about and said, "That's a Chinese proverb."

And one of them continued, "I would never have amounted to anything if it were not for adversity."

With that, Mary squinted and seriously scanned in all directions, for context, for stagecraft, theatrical cues, for show controls or a playwright-associated metathetic stub, such as a hidden stub or sunken empire, to reemerge then says, "That's J.C. Penney" and resolved the problem with a crisp twenty dollar bill, closed the door, and mumbled in absolute disbelief, as well as grumped, "J.C. Penney, really?"

That was then.

She says, "Or it might be a server, yes, someone delivering a legal notice, a lawsuit notification or court order, and likely the mansion foreclosure, with additional documents to trash credit ratings, as well as press forward on all possible fronts, well, to guarantee a full and systematic destruction of Agrippa, yes," and eyes narrow.

Regardless, Mary stumbles down the mansion hallway, then room after room.

However she stops at the front doors and carefully peeks out one side window after another.

Yet she sees no one, and hears nothing, not even as an ear presses to a door here and there.

Then she considers the unthinkable, "a punch, yes, open the door and deliver" a quick superwoman punch, deliver a fist, a fistic event, a solid punch to the face, the type where a person might reel and spit out a few bloody teeth, or better yet, become a feeble drool, "a feeble empire, and mumble," such as a person or organization that would mostly sit and drool in one form or another, then once in a while have a wild-eyed-fully-animated notion, yet cannot articulate a clear line of effort, and that effort contains very active and colorful delirium, of gestic hallucinations, delusions, disorganizations and confusions about preposition, postposition and circumposition. Then the articulation slows to muddled speech, about very complex content, about the next great Zeitgeist or major breakthrough, such as a major mystery, an unsolved problem in physics, mathematics, chemistry, biology, medicine, or about Ludwig Wittgenstein notebooks, or third culture kid, equilibrium types or leaky abstractions. Then as the vital revelation nears, that person reaches a great mental barrier, realizes it then rants with delirium at the wilderness, at the frontier, and that person seems trapped in that endless cycle, of a person kept as a garden vegetable, a trial garden, "yes," from a fistic.

Then she says with quiet determination, "Regardless, forget all of that, scrub from the mind, really scrub from the mental conversation pit, an exedra, and better yet, a single punch which knocks that person out of the timeline, out of history, and into forever, such as sail away.

"Yes" and the eyes narrow.

# CHAPTER  18

So, she prepares to open a door, and braces herself with a well-placed foot, for a tremendous effort then snarls, and repeatedly readies her best fist for a Sunday punch, then practices the oh-so-spectacular motion several times, to warm up, to get ready and deliver it just right, and with considerable power that would produce an instant knockout, and the type that a recipient would collapse straight down into an ugly heap—"Yes."

And as the door slowly opens, Mary makes subtle adjustments, moves the hips to maximize readiness, as well as the ability to leverage power—full power.

So, she moves into the best possible position and angle.

Then the quintessential "It Girl" appears, Vay, from that initial ill-fated mansion fundraiser, one of those people that can go by one name.

And memories return of this woman, memories of that event, which had two very important functions, a charity fundraiser to auction donated haute couture outfits, with the proceeds supporting a noble cause, and Agrippa would meet her banker to secure a mortgage for this mansion.

Of equal importance, this woman represents everyone's first choice, the unattainable, the one people want to be near yet cannot have and must settle for a substitute, settle on a less than ideal choice.

She generates real buzz.

And when this person moves through a crowd, social eddies swirl and pull people neatly to and fro, as if aftermath, similar to the hydrodynamics simulation pattern of the Rayleigh–Taylor instability, that swirl of turmoil, byproduct and distribution, and so on—as the process takes on a certain style.

Then here and now, the worst thing happens, Mary arrives face to face then self-arrests in a state of babble, as if a goofy cliché, or a silly, carefree, such as once she departs, Mary will want to kick herself, and go on and on about the stupid and out-of-character things she said and did.

Right now, Mary alternates between babble, giddy and a homespun impish demeanor, that cycle.

And with a single touch to Mary's shoulder, Vay transmutes her mind.

So much so in distinct stages, she settles, and eventually regains her normal disposition then provides a full babysitting orientation, a complete tour, well, a less than forthcoming version, the official version regarding this unconscious red-haired man, who resembles a Thracian, a freed man, a peltast, such as an Agrianian peltast.

Afterwards, she expresses her heartfelt thanks and solemnly promises to return Sunday morning, well before Agrippa arrives late Sunday evening, which represents more than enough time to insure an ever so smooth transition.

Then Mary departs.

However regarding Vay, the word spreads.

It spreads, as those types of things rarely remain a secret.

And exactly two hours later, uninvited people arrive at the mansion, a few here and there.

In fact, they enter the driveway and exits cars, which reveal all types of people in a wide range of outfits, even slumber wear, 1950's cocktail, high tea and princess for a day.

Of course Vay immediately phones Mary, yet no answer.

So she leaves one urgent message after another, as a considerable number of people enter through various doors, even a sliding door.

Eventually vast numbers arrive, and they surge inside.

Then one brightly labeled tour bus after another enters the driveway and parks in neat rows then world-renowned bands arrive, which includes rock, pop, as well as folk music, and they stretch for relief, really stretch, in search of satisfaction.

So much so an arm reaches, really reaches, and trunk twists here and there then leg extends for the best technique.

And what is the best stretch technique after a long sit?

What represents the best method to find real relief, as well as satisfaction then a mellow well-being glow?

And eventually, they look about and marvel at the estate, the setting, at picturesque gardens of colorful bloom, as well as shrubs, subshrubs, and especially herbal plants, a virtuous treatise of medicinal, tonic, culinary and aromatic expressions, and far more than what one might expect within the golden age of classical and Renaissance gardens. Where a person can sit within philosophical secular or sacred space then absorb apotropaic, transformative, and regenerative powers of a pristine place, a place vivid, vital, free and fair, a place wholly natural and absolutely fascinating. A special place artists, poets, and scholars can sit then daydream venture, yes, and let the mind wander to solve some great mystery, or mentally drift, such as drift on an ever so slow wave.

All this gives the place a certain image of prosperity, progress and peace, a place in full accord with nature, as if it represents an unofficial paradise, a place that might lead into the transcendent, might trigger a full restoration of glory, the original long-lost glory now found.

The guests notice, scan, seriously consider and absorb the charm, and it activates their full imagination, especially from an adventurous footpath that leads to one not-so-secret garden after another, an st-connectivity, context-free grammar or Risch algorithm field, a cultivated crop, a trial garden, and each garden with a microclimate, as well as stylistic allure, with full potential, where some appear spacious, grand, and noble.

A person can sit in one of many small niches, such as inside a small bamboo grove, or under the full protection of a weeping willow in bloom, or between huge ceremonial boulder crops, as if an ancient rock culture, an elaborate prehistoric tribute, which form a poetic megalithic boulder garden shrine that enables rare and sacred space to form, and where anyone of these places, a person might sit, meditate, and ponder the great mysteries of the universe, as an explorer, third culture person, psychonautic, transformative, grok or kythe agent, or equilibrium refinement then notice something special, notice special-purpose districts.

Meanwhile, groupies follow, gush and fawn.

Eventually word reaches Tommy, Benny then Emma.

As a result they immediately fly into action and drive to the mansion.

Not much later, Reece and Vera hear through another channel and they stumble into action, followed by Zoey and Mel.

Meanwhile at the mansion, luxury cars park everywhere, Bentley Continental Flying Spur, Bentley Continental GT, Rolls Royce Ghost, Rolls Royce Phantom, Bentley Continental Super Sport, Maybach 62, as well as Mercedes-Benz S-Class, Aston Martin, Maserati, BMW, a wide variety of luxury SUV/Crossovers, and other Veblens, other conspicuous consumption of superior socioeconomic status, as well as Giffens.

And the people less likely to arrive in a Giffen do, such as people with real wealth, with old money, quite, along with the not so, people of average wealth yet remarkable taste, for example that superior skill of a true tastemaker, a person who decides the next great fashion trend.

Of which it seems quite a remarkable sight of luxury, and among them sit a Giffen, plain old car or worn-out pickup truck, a hunk of junk, the type of vehicle that truly belongs in a junkyard yet sits next to the a masterpiece, such as what one expects at Pebble Beach *Concours d'Elegance*.

And oddly enough, no one seems to mind, not the elite owners or Bubba.

Well, you would think it might cause a serious look, as well as tension, and yet the opposite, as people seem quite reasonable.

In fact, they seem civil, as if a civic virtue, and this place represents a republic of virtue, of charm, such as extraordinary style, elegance, charm, of full potential, as if a plurisubharmonic function, or unlimited superior of complex analytic space.

Then more people arrive, which include members of the Chambre Syndicale de la Haute Couture, one official, two correspondents and one guest member, followed by well-known socialites, a few British and French nobles with titles, as well as shakers, movers, hedge fund managers, venture capitalists and bankers, as a small number of key aids trail behind and struggle to catch up.

And all the while, supercilious fashionistas nitpick, animate and roll their eyes, then meticulously mock and find pleasure in doing so.

In fact, they point, snicker, gossip, and peck, then beam with pride as if they won a Nobel Prize for solving a monumental blight.

Of the gal pals, Samantha arrives first, followed by Quinn.

However, by then theme parties and events are well underway throughout the mansion and on all floors, even in private quarters.

Of equal importance, each party and event has a substantial life of its own, as people move about in strange outfits quite appropriate to the room.

And throughout the mansion, world-famous bands discreetly play in various sections, and they do so as an exclusive, by invitations-only to exceptional crowds, and not a typical invitation, but with a rare protocol, a secret method not quite evident, yet after an elaborate set of topical questions as well as the correct garb, a person might enter, and elite wealth appears to have no significant special privilege.

Although it appears to help in some cases, especially real wealth, old money—very, enormous wealth, and not a new age version, or first-, second- or third-generation money—not the modern version, as in modernism with that restless examination and experimentation of every aspect of life in search of better way, and all that wasteful effort, and not a pretend wealthy with special looks and techniques.

Rather, it helps entering if these people have a considerable fortune earned with an exceptional style, earned with a certain culture, intellect and wit, especially a remarkable wit, as well as done so with a certain bearing and precept that creates high honors along with a remarkable degree of ethos or guiding beliefs and ideals.

Yet it by no means guarantees the ability to enter any one of these exclusives, especially if a guest fails that elaborate set of topical questions, as well as wears an incorrect garb.

Again, exceptions exist.

Eventually, Karm arrives, and heads turn as people whisper, consider the full implications and wonder who will have the courage to approach with appropriate questions.

Elsewhere in the mansion, a few discreet operas begin, which include *Don Giovanni*, *Orphée aux enfers*, *Dafne*, *Aida*, as well as *The Marriage of Figaro* in full licentious form.

In fact, in each room, nearly everyone is period-correct with costumes, manner and speech, except for an occasional redneck, manga Greek style, Stilyaga, Gopnik, member of a lost generation, hipster, and a few redshirts.

Surprisingly enough, and not in a period-correct costume, no one concerns, as they fit neatly inside the setting, the atmospherics.

Needless to say, wave after wave of gal pals arrive—Tommy, Benny, Emma, Reece, Vera, Zoey and Mel.

They enter the mansion; look about, stand thunderstruck then try to restore order to what seems unstoppable.

Moments later Seska arrives.

# CHAPTER 19

The gal pals have great difficulty entering certain events, certain exclusives by invitations only, as they seem wholly unaware of the protocol, that secret method, which requires an elaborate set of topical questions as well as period-correct garb, plus something else not quite apparent.

And they try answering questions, and, well, get an A for effort.

However each tests proves quite difficult.

Although with a special breathing technique, a minor congressional aide named Gus enters.

In fact he easily moves through one exclusive event after another in search of something.

And he ascribes to a golden rule of never underestimate the power of anonymity, and the ability to hide in plain sight, especially when maneuvering among people with enormous wealth, influence, privilege, position, reputation and connection, and of equal importance, never underestimate the addictive impulse created by power, money, and fame.

That minor congressional aide specializes in anonymity and the discreet application of.

One of the most difficult skill sets to acquire and deftly apply in life, truly a lost art, to have enormous power, influence, connection, as well as remain vital, and yet barely visible, such as the type of person with very little backstory and a keen ability to keep it that way, with a discreet craft of appearance and movement—in fact, ordinary, a nondescript person, and yet, fully and deftly in control with the ability to steer events through subtle hint and movement, which burrow into the subconscious of others, and eventually trigger a plan, path, and action.

Put another way, and for lack of a better phrase, this style or technique by Gus has a Jedi mind trick aspect, though more similar to a liminal master of ceremony, for the phase transition, and with far more nuance, and very little to do with a mimic instruction. As he deploys some type of metaphysical and universal shared wave system, maybe with technology, which ritualized space and focal point, as if he and participants are one and the same for those brief moments, yet participants do not know it, and something partially described with the concept of atonement and being at one, a function of harmonics.

All of which regarding Gus, might start with some type of well-timed ritualized quiet and barely detectable breathing trick, presence, mood, mindset, as well as subtle clues vaguely similar to Anapanasati and a few other old-school systems.

Is it a religious tool or device, or secular, such as technology-based, which activates the fundamental laws of biology, chemistry, economics or systems in general?

Regardless of the mechanics, this trick or technique by Gus seems to evoke a heuristic event, a speedup effect and decision shortcut, which in retrospect, gives the appearance of a deliberation process that feels cautious, prudent, clear, efficient, effective, practical, as well as a decisive application of power, yet leaves no significant trace of the source—all of which comes across as a true lost art.

Then here and now, it becomes quite clear, Gus carefully moves towards a patrician who watches *Orphée aux enfers*, the same German, the one who owns a garden-mansion quite similar to *Grüneburgschlößchen*, Frankfurt, one of the many Rothschild-style mansions, with various features a person might expect in a secular temple if you will, or *tome*, a sacred precinct with special rules, and surrounded by an extraordinary forty-acre garden. In fact, a picturesque place of colorful bloom, which includes special shrubs, subshrubs, and herbal plants, yet not a virtuous treatise of medicinal, tonic, culinary and aromatic expressions, nevertheless what one might expect within the golden age of classical and Renaissance gardens, and not a Gilded Age version, the *nouveau* riche.

Elsewhere and moments later, Livia dressed as *Marie de' Medici*, Mero as *Averardo de' Medici,* and a scientist dressed as *Francesco I de' Medici* enter the mansion, and with ease they move through the Great Hall, Ladies' Reception Room then settle in the Music Room, yet often eye *Albizzi* and *Strozzi*, as the opera *Dafne* begins.

And gal pals perplex on how most people freely move from room to room yet bodyguards prevent others.

Of equal importance, each guard resembles a mountain of humanity, huge, burly, and one buttermilk biscuit short of 300 pounds, as men with no neck, barrel chest, and a massive back.

As well, they resemble men who shave early morning, yet have a five o'clock shadow by noon, and yet wear an impeccably tailored suit made with the finest materials, as if they were a true classic in their own right, which really puzzles the gal pals, especially Benny.

Just as importantly, and when need be, they menace with a respectable snarl, eyes bulge and square jaws clench then they flash a steely look, a refined temper version, all of which comes across as quite menacing, yet ever so cultured, and enough so, the ladies, the gal pals back up again, and again to a safe distance.

And yet Benny does not, and smiles, in fact beams, and sees the very best in these people—and the best in people in general, sees their full potential. All of which translates into a personality of someone who, well, should have been the mother of civilization, someone alert, inclusive, serene, and fascinated by truly great mysteries.

However, her charm does not improvement the situation, and these men show no interest, as well as seem quite devoted to the containment of each event, that strategy, policy and structure to maintain a certain balance overall mood or atmosphere.

Of equal note or greater, and about eight miles away, Mary returns to the mansion early, and drives through a pristine old-growth temperate coniferous forests of cedar, yew, cypress, spruce, fir, juniper and pine.

And along the way, she sees neat poetic bars of sunlight that beam through picturesque forest foliage, a place that seems eternal and timeless, as if Arcadia unspoiled, a harmonious wilderness of solitude, spirit yet with culture.

And this exceptional place has no theatrical criticism, no criticism and controversy, no controversy over linguistic and ethnic identity, no lost state of innocent, no fall of human species, no disobedience, guilt and shame, well, as she drives a narrow sign-free mountain road that tightly winds about, where a single lane shares both traffic directions.

Eventually, this car exits a tree grove then enters ancient woodland, a majestic mystery with a patch of fog here and there.

Then the car moves through another pristine old growth forest of yew, spruce, fir, juniper, and pine.

And about 800 feet from the sculpted thirty-two-foot high iron mansion gates and limestone wall bordering the property, she stops.

Well, because cars sit on each side of the road, and all the way to those gates.

Of equal importance, chauffeurs mingle.

A few offer her shrugs, to reflect their frustration as well, and convey the need to, well; simply make the best of it.

However moments later, they notice something ahead, squint, realize, huddle and point to a free space much closer to the gate then eagerly direct her into this tight yet doable spot.

Although it requires parallel parking, in fact an advanced skill, something Mary never mastered.

Regardless, she tries and tries.

Of which, it consists mostly of a start and abrupt stop, of one near-miss after another.

"Oops!

"Sorry!

"Oh my!" and one word not fit for print.

Oddly enough, these people seem more than patient, show helpful hand signs to direct, and say such things as "Whoa!

"Backup.

"Stop!

"Go forward.

"Now turn left.

"No, your other left.

"Easy does it.

"Slowly, turn the wheel counterclockwise.

"No, turn the other version of counterclockwise.

"Good, easy.

"OK.

"Stop!

"No, try again," that pattern.

And she nearly gouges a Maybach 62 then Mercedes-Benz S-Class, Aston Martin and pickup truck.

Again and oddly enough, no one seems to mind, the chauffeurs, elite owners or Bubba.

Then more drivers approach her, as well as honored guests, and they politely offer directions, which gives the full impression of a major event yet quite civil, as if a civic virtue, and this place represents a republic of virtue, then of charm and clever wit, quite, such as extraordinary style, elegance, charm, of full as well as true human potential, the best of the best, as if a plurisubharmonic function, or unlimited superior of complex analytic space, of proper art and communications.

However, to her, the parking space seems too small, very, yet the crowd encourages another effort, and this time, "relax."

"Yes, relax.

"Don't take it so personal.

"Practice your breathing.

"Don't overthink.

"Become one with the car.

"Exactly, try, yes, try a meditation.

"Rest on each moment.

"Don't think of your trouble tree.

"Rest when trouble arrives, relax, really relax and breathe."

Even Bubba agrees, as well as shows one advanced breathing technique after another, shows Buddhism, Vedic, Christian and Chinese in great detail, and seems more than willing to express the twenty-three known methods.

However, the risk of damage to those exceptional cars causes fear beyond reason and debate.

And it causes her to stop, completely surrender, lower the head, and vent a long burst of air.

Then moments someone sees an even better parking space, closer, and with more room to maneuver.

So they encourage her forward, which she begrudgingly does and the polite instructions continue.

"Whoa!

"Backup.

"Stop!

"Go forward.

"Now turn left.

"No, your other left.

"Easy does it.

"Slowly, turn the wheel counterclockwise.

"No, turn the other version of counterclockwise.

"Good, easy, OK.

"Stop!

"No try again," that pattern.

This time she nearly gouges a Bentley Continental GT, Rolls Royce Ghost, Rolls Royce Phantom, and Giffen on one side of the road, then Maybach 62, Bentley Continental Super Sport, Maserati, BMW, luxury SUV/Crossover, and Yugo on the other side, and again.

So much so to her, the risk and pressure seems tremendous, especially to these Pebble Beach *Concours d'Elegance* quality cars.

And eventually she completely surrender, lower the head and vent a long burst of air.

However, the crowd would have none of that, the civic virtue, in a republic of virtue, such as extraordinary style, elegance, and charm of true human potential.

So they offer encouragement, as *The Dresser*, a support system, a spokesperson for the self, or as a host, a master of ceremonies or *compère* for the self, to bestow stature, value, and virtue.

Of which in stages, she absorbs and the posture improves.

So much so, she eventually completes the park then seems quite surprised, well, with the ease of entering that space, as well as the fact that she did not hit the Bentley Continental GT, Rolls Royce Ghost, Rolls Royce Phantom, or Giffen.

Meanwhile the mansion events continue, which she hears, turns and oddly enough shows no rage, no flash of a temper, clenched jaw or readied fists, and no pacing about, bulging eyes, foaming at the mouth, no rubbing the neck in absolute disbelief and anguish, no knot in the stomach pit, and no feeling of vengeance best served cold.

Instead, something else happens.

Mary has a keen interest, a fascination with this process, and the fine details of civic virtue, a republic of virtue, a keen interest in things most people overlook, take for granted.

Well, because it seems quite fascinating, the swirl of activity, those people, events and especially the relationships between, between what should contain a complex schism, a cultural divide in various traditions, particularly the bitterness and animosity between normal human factions, between cultural subsets, which most often extend quite deep.

So, she dispassionately studies and has no impulse to feral-leap or nip at guest, just tremendous curiosity about the group members, dynamics and metrics, the science of.

As a result, she says to the uniformed chauffeurs, "Sounds like a nice party."

And they chime together in full agreement then defer to a portly fellow named Sauvignon, who seems a bit odd, in a disheveled way, the ill-fitting outfit as well as role, oversize, yet under he has a certain flair, a style guide, such as a guide open source higher-order function, no, wait, a special reference guide, a Zen survivor yet good shepherd.

So he steps forward and appears as if a walking-wobble, such as bad feet or shoes.

And yes, the shoes, quite, well-worn as well as often repaired without the aid of a professional, with a best effort of materials that seem close yet not quite, which, with other clues implies much of his life has been that of a genuine itinerant, similar a hobo yet more sophisticated, such as a Bohemian, and not quite a perpetual traveler; nor Leatherman.

Yet he has a special something, and regardless, the type of person the Nazis would force to wear a black triangle badge on his clothing, well, because he did not neatly fit into the machine.

Many places in the Deep South would jail this type of person, quickly, especially in a small town controlled by a stark system, a rigid and absolute, a harsh and blunt style, for example black or white as if shades of grey, subtle things and a complex system seriously irritate them, complex categories irritate; so, get to a point quickly or else, such as fight, flight or surrender, those limited choices.

Other cultures have a similar version, a version of the truth, subjective and justification; such as justify a state or estate, for example a medieval literary "estate satire," an oppressive draconian or more, or a Athenian law scribe technique, who for a small offense writes a heavy punishment, as if a cottage industry, a way to earn money and power, a way to build a truly great civilization, which gives the impression of cruel and unusual, a history of the human species, especially to an outsider, to someone not acclimated to so many incremental steps beyond a bright red line of reasonable, of true civility.

These places often have a large-and-in-charge, or Mr. Big, or Miss Big, or the man or woman behind the man, and they often take great pride in punishment, as well as a lack system alternatives, lack real choice, other ways of thinking, and if capable, they would dropped a building on someone, or some other public lesson.

He appears self-taught, mellow and quite civil.

Apparently, a shortage of qualified drivers exists, especially for these events, a shortage beyond the first, second, and third choices.

Of equal significance, Sauvignon seems quite pleased and wobbles forward to speak for them, which they nod in full agreement as he says, "What we have here is another extraordinary event.

"These are some of the most diverse theme parties ever.

"They have an extraordinary setup, world-class musicians that include rock, folk, hill country blues, and yes, opera," he says as his eyes widen in admiration.

Then he leans towards her to confide a certain truth, "If done correctly, opera can transform."

She says in a subtle way, as if to gently unlock a door, "Really? "How so?"

And with that, Sauvignon seriously considers, then his demeanor generates a smile that radiates and he says, "At its worst, which is often, opera is a bunch of overly costumed people, mostly heavyset in a braying event, driving people away, causing them to consider fleeing to a distant land, such as a barren island, or desolate desert plateau, or stark Alpine tundra, or onto the remote Eurasian Steppe to gain relief.

"A bad opera drives people away; which is most opera.

"However, at its finest, it frees the soul, and you soar free and true into a better existence, and with a certain dignity of spirit, as well as exceptionalism, the way it was supposed to be, beyond time and space as ethereal, as an ethereal specie, and above it all with boundless possibility, above the naturally-occurring demiplanes, and as if a dream proto realm yet the loft creates reality, creates fact, creates a better place true, free and fair.

"And dread naught.

"So much so it conveys a restoration, the way it should have been all along and in the beginning, then can reveals a theory of everything, the ultimate theory, the all-inclusive explanation of the universe, of life, as well as what a person might expect within the golden age of the classical and Renaissance, Renaissance Humanism, Neoclassicism and the Age of Enlightenment, and the Romantic era version, a full restoration of glory, the original long-lost glory now found, opera.

"Moreover, it does so as if a universal wave of destiny.

"Yes, this represents opera, at its best.

"It can open one door after another, as well as the eternal, and offer true nobility, and act as a vehicle into the transcendent, into rarified space."

Then he checks his watch and says, "Eight, seven, six," and the woman called Cub arrives from nowhere, wearing that elaborate basket thing, as well as a period-correct costume and mask to fully disguise her frame of mind, the frame-shift narrative process, "Three, two, one."

Moments later, Cub and Sauvignon sing a duet, a world-class aria, and this expressive melody seems quite remarkable, as well as matches the exact secretive performance underway inside the mansion, second floor, in what might be room numbered 206 yet none of the rooms have numbers.

As a result, drivers gaze at this heartfelt performance, "of opera, and human destiny, to free the soul, and soar into a better place, a better existence, and with a certain dignity of spirit, as well as exceptionalism, the way it was supposed to be, beyond time and space as ethereal, as an ethereal specie, and above it all with boundless possibility, above the naturally-occurring demiplanes, and as if a dream proto realm yet the loft creates reality, creates fact, creates a better place true, free and fair.

"And dread naught."

And afterwards, Cub exits just as quietly as she arrived.

Eventually, Sauvignon slips of out that mindstream on the edge of forever, turns and says, "Opera, at its best," then takes a transitional step away from opera and "What can I sing?

"The very best of Michael Littwin?

"Yes, *Oh Danny Boy*,

"It's you, it's you must go and I must bide," then he sings.

# CHAPTER 20

At the same time, elsewhere, and because of entanglement, Agrippa startles then buckles to one knee, and midway through that song, the third of four iron bands restricting her heart releases, a mental construct, restriction; an ever so stale script.

So much so and eventually, the air seems fresh, such as "sae fresh and fair."

And with each deep breath, she notices the difference then admires the clear, cloudless and serene day, as well as basks in warm sunlight as the eyes close.

Then each breath renews and relaxes, which causes the mind to drift, yes; relax and drift.

Then she imagines an ever so soft landing at day's end, with head a comfy pillow, yes, in a garden hammock surrounded by colorful and fragrant bloom, surrounded by the recuperative aspect of nature, of sae fresh and fair.

Eventually, her thoughts focus on that overgrown mansion garden, and the way it was supposed to be in the beginning, with a swirl of new ideas, possibilities, expansion and events.

And in that garden setting, the Renaissance, Renaissance Humanism, Neoclassicism, Age of Enlightenment, she would basks in warm sunlight, in truth, beauty and mysterious beam of completeness, of totality, a peaceful majestic glory, and become a fully realized redemption, and the source of a great culture, become the source of a truly great civilization, as well as create a mental vapor, the atmospherics, and ethereal vivid universal dream of a psychonautic that sails through distinguished states, properties, and *sui generis* sae fresh and fair.

Elsewhere, as the song ends, Mary thanks Sauvignon and others for their help then continues toward the mansion, and carefully studies things along the way, especially car after car neatly parked, and passes one buzz of people after another, passes each swirl then lone person here and there.

And once inside the mansion, unfamiliar faces greet her as if best friend for life, for life, liberty, and the pursuit of happiness.

Yet no one seems remotely familiar; however people offer ever so polite small talk, libation and directions to exclusive events, as if exclusive federal powers and abilities.

And these people seem more than willing to confide, especially to her, their long-lost friend, and explain the system in great detail, what they learned over a lifetime, as well as whisper the secret password system to a hard-earned exclusive.

To Mary, this gives the place a unique feel, an exceptional place, of being home yet as an ultimate insider, and what they must know, experience, and benefit.

And yet she recognizes no one, not even with a squint, one angle after another, as that often happens. A person meets at a certain angle, such as face-to-face or in a specific situation with content, with certain cues.

And without those clues, the person or situation remains a mystery, in this case a cabal, secret society, and in some cases a mystery-*bouffe*.

So she maintains a poker face to explore each and every aspect, then mingles with a special style, as an exclusive, a *sprezzatura*, a certain nonchalance, well, to conceal all art, all vital thoughts and mission regardless of each situation, which will give the full appearance of effortless and without telling thoughts, such a poker tell, and "Really?"

As well as she shows an easy facility, especially when asked about difficult subjects, quite, and things no human other than the ultimate insiders would know or try to solve, and she often accomplishes the difficult action with subtle gesture or two, as if to hide much of the consciousness activity, hide thought construct methods, such as techniques of her contemplative tree, the deliberation process, and metacognition, about when and how to use a particular strategy.

And when pressed, she also does so with an ever so smooth irony or quick wit, a clever and effortless construct, which disguises real desires, feelings, thinking procedures, means, and intent behind a mask of reticence and nonchalance much of the time.

Then she moves from group to group, listens and learns more about each one, and carefully studies who orbits what.

One group after another contains elite patricians, socialites, tastemakers, as well as a superstar diva, prima donna, divo, primo uomo all-stars and with a grand on- and off-stage personality, with style, with an ever so special flair.

Moreover, they continue to alternate with praise, sips of spirit, and breath, as well as seem ever so fascinated, because of the various ultrarare groups, symmetry, due proportions, set construction, moduli space, in addition to the extensive travel circuit potentials, especially the new people and communities. As that represents one of the most difficult processes, to add just the right new people, add a fresh perspective, beyond their normal annual migration route, beyond the traditional pattern, beyond the World Economic Forum, Milken Institute Global conference, Allen & Company conference, TED and dreary Foggy Bottom meetings said vital, beyond those predictable meetings, with so many very needy politicians. Such as the professional panderer and climber who each struggle four hours a day in their own private yet party boiler room, in a phone booth or slightly larger, struggle for direct solicitations, of dialing for dollars, well, as the handler secretly records, which to some people feel as if just another cult, yes, a cult, an *argumentum ad hominem*, based on a stale script, a logical fallacy, a dusty creed, that uses an ever so shallow language game, such as a stale process. While powers-that-be create yet another tempest, for what feels as if an endless number of, to fix or prevent a self-made crisis? All of which in fact appears to offer a side benefit, of build a resume, find a future job slot as a proxy for a competing power, for too-big-to-fail, and find an ever so soft landing, into luxury, "Yes, ah," such as a skybox, or lower, such as a niche among chaos, the modern version of Dante's *Vita Nuova* and *Divina Commedia*?

Here and now, these hedge fund managers and venture capitalists mumble, "Thank God," or some other cultural equivalent, less jet traffic, especially for private jets, and where to park them close to these events, as things have escalated beyond reason, such as the Super Bowl, Masters Golf Tournament, Wimbledon, Monaco Grand Prix, Concours d'Elegance, Royal Ascot, Triple Crown, and the four fashion world capitals of "Milan, Paris, New York, and London," as well as "Portugal, Rome, São Paulo, and Berlin" and the food and wine festival migration, which includes Aspen, South Beach, San Diego, White Truffle and other premier events, with an ever so brief stop at the Cannes Film Festival then devote far more time at Cannes Lions International Festival of Creativity. As those travel circuits, those often elusive searches, represent a considerable effort, to find the right crowd, in the ideal circuit, such as private, inclusive, discreet, as well as discrete, such as a safe haven, sanctuary, and maybe *A Home in the Meadow*, someplace elsewhere, and "Away, away, come away with me," that search, that elusive circuit, which mysteriously shifts, and is never quite the same. "Why?" And yet, once there, it resembles a great nexus of rare space, of warmth, inclusive, free and fair, of "Away, away, come away with me."

# CHAPTER 21

Here and now, Mary neatly moves through one tight pack then another unusual cluster of people, a transformative star-making system, an event, the studio system in action, and major studios, that process, and a rare look behind the curtain so to speak, at the methods, the ways and means, and those industry secrets, as all industries have special technique and process or more, and hidden behind a closed door or two.

And standing next to a bay window, Mary sees in great detail the sequence of events, the small talk, as well as intermediate, advanced, and ultimate talk, such as if you own them, you somehow now own that industry, for example when a lowly actor suddenly has the "it factor," and becomes the *de facto* boss of a major organization, a too-big-to-fail, and in this case a major studio, and is now at the center of an organization, with a sudden flip, yet this person never moved from that seat, which has now become in the seat of power, true power, and now a tastemaker who can command that genre, that surge of power with real implications.

Especially once that scene ends.

And all scenes end, such as end the feud, or escalate, yes, escalate, and the end-Botomian mass extinction, and become a fossil, petrify into a rock, that end-user's license agreement, or approaches this rock, closer, yes, and still closer to get within prime time striking distance then seriously consider delivering one spinning thunderous chop after another, and another to pulverize it into smithereens, into rubble and a cloud of dust.

Then here and now, a lull arrives, a pause in the conversation, a natural break, as if part of segment, a branch, and in need of a decision, such as a pathway, and come away with me, a fresh start, a new beginning, a new way of life out of the quagmire.

Yet here and now, the "it" person could say a crude remark, well, that leaves considerable damage, such as build a new industry by destroying the old, and major sections of, aspects thought dated, stale, an industry drag, such as on profits, and now a reason to cut a few segments, "yes, right here and now," that impulse, that snap decision, which can effect so many people, as well as communities, of cut loose, and away.

# CHAPTER

That type of mansion conversational lull arrives, a pause, as if a vacuum, such as a door opens with an opportunity for change or continue same-old-same-old, for example, double down.

And outside the bay window in stealth, a distinguished and differentiated subspace domain, a rock creature smolders as well as monitors that meeting and thinks these major movie studios need a change, and Hollywood, that industry and region needs something, as well as the human species and social constructs.

*And what do they need?*

*What is right or wrong with the current studio system?*

*What does it lack, and why?*

*What are the differences between now and the golden age?*

And this rare look behind the curtain as well as conversational pause *reveals a major identity crisis, of what have they become?*

*Where are the new movie masterpieces, such as those made during the Golden Age of Hollywood, those epic movies, as well as timeless, awe-inspiring, ambitious, and soul-searching?*

*The community seems exhausted from the relentless daily grind, from the exhaustive process of smoothing and refurbishing so many bad scripts as well as shot movies, of meeting after meeting, and rule by committee, by institution.*

*And when will relief arrive from average, from making average movies, making dull predictable, which seems so loud and artificial from computer-generated imagery?*

*When did artificial become the norm, such as fake, for example a fake script, as well predicament, emotion, action, explosion, and debris?*

*Why do they use so many fake sounds, fake noises in general, especially fake laughs, as a true laugh represents a critical event in life, to feel alive, so why fake one of the most important aspects of human existence?*

*OK-OK, some people prefer artificial flowers and plants, such as the dandelion, borage, basil, goldenrod, aster, common yarrow, and purple coneflower, or honeybee favorite colors, such as blue and yellow, ones to stop, smell, consider and meticulously gathering essentials, as well as eternals, and so with a remarkable similarity to ones described in the Atharvaveda, and at Delphi, as well as described by Aristotle, Plato, Virgil, Seneca, Erasmus, and Tolstoy.*

*And some people like a fake Rolex or designer goods, the best of the best, or best of a bad situation, such as life in a trap, a quandary.*

*However, why built an industry on that, such as a major movie studio, which seems quite similar to what other social constructs do, as the phenomenon appears in so many other systems?*

*Why create so many average big-budget blockbusters and already-established franchises that way?*

*And the next expensive blockbuster always reminds the audience of the last blockbuster, such as bigger and louder, as well as the last sequel, adaptation and formula which have a built-in audience.*

*Well, the process eventually resembles an entertainment factory, or life in an institution? And movies seem average on purpose, and lack a good story for a reason, of commerce versus art, especially in this era of big data, that pull, and of a script revised by editor teams, who carefully study analytics, analytic–synthetic distinction, a priori, a posteriori, of two-dimensions, well, especially as it related to the private viewing system, such as in Orange County and other test markets for feedback?*

*Is the system average on purpose, run-of-the-mill, of good enough, well, to not only please consumers but to condition, create then support them, to create a new reality, a new type of consumer or market, such as a boffo simulation, such as look successful, well, because image is just as important as reality?*

*What is wrong with a fake Rolex or fake designer good?*

*And when will the golden age of Hollywood return, the next Kondratiev wave, a super cycle segment, the next great surge on the long wave?*

*Or will it ignore the fundamental rules of nature, system, symmetry, symbiosis, "set and setting," as in the term to trip, really trip, and trip into a theater of the truly absurd.*

*And sometimes, a truly great experiment goes wrong, really wrong, yes. Where enterprise or some other social construct creates a magnificent curiosity, maybe a system, and something that gives the full impression of true glory, and yet quite artificial, where a creature or thing is so far ahead of the curve, so far beyond foresight, and before the powers-that-be realized the full potential and implications.*

*So much so, the device or system gains control over the creator, and not vice versa, which conveys the full impression of a situational irony from people, well, who ignored the fundamental principles of nature, and in this case create entertainment so advance, complex, compelling, and ever changing that it becomes the master, as in the real science of a truly powerful master, a similar theme and variation of Voyager, The Thaw, yet in this case they do not realize it, and think of it as just another experiment, another tool or system.*

# CHAPTER 23

Meanwhile, here and now at the mansion event, that transformative star-making system, the studio system in process, and Mary studies their dilemma then heated debate, and at the next natural pause she moves from one mansion event after another, and passes one very unusual person after another.

And yet, she carefully studies and does so without revealing her purpose, her mission since discovering these major mansion events.

As she whispers to herself, "It was supposed to be another quiet weekend, such as in the morning, rise late, yes, rollover, maybe a few times then eventually go to one nursing class after another, yet take it easy, breathe, relax, maybe coast into the classroom setting, yes, and sit, as well as close the eyes and relax, especially as a beam of sunlight bathes, that type of opportunity, and maybe *A Home in the Meadow*, someplace elsewhere, and "Away, away, come away with me."

However here and now, she has hard-earned momentum, inertia, as this mansion has so many exclusives, and she must study as many as possible to find the event organizer, the source of this property abuse, such as who has the audacity, temerity, and chutzpah, the supreme self-confidence to host all these events, and over the past weekends.

In addition, she must not become trapped in any given situation, in an exclusive, as each one has a certain gravitas.

And of greater importance, she must avoid being exposed as a great pretender.

Such as, these people might realize who she really is, realize her real potential.

Or just as important, if a person looks in the mirror at just the right moment and angle, they might see the true self; see a lost opportunity at a major threshold, or reference point indentation, or reference class problem. Yet that person quickly hides among the scripts, or quickly picks a script, then acts, and often with a very fake manner, as the great pretender.

Or late night, this person can sit under the stars, among true greatness, the aesthetic, or wherever the daily slog eventually leads to, such as no more excuses, and why make more excuses for the self, or life in general, for nature, why grade it on curve, a bell-shaped curve, an education term for "Oh my, such a slow learner!" in fact dense, or said another way, a sluggish, obtuse and foolish mind or the universal collective mind, the universe, such as the over and under soul, that type of realization.

And ponder that, or better yet, the next *zeitgeist* if you will, or *weltgeist*, then do one's duty regardless, such as formulate the ability to determine a nation, or determine an era, or, okay, settle for a classic alcohol buzz, to numb the trouble tree, the mind, mental baggage, or numb a persistent personal demon, a tenacious pest, as if a nuisance tax, and during a circadian rhythm triple witching hour from melatonin, liquor, and habit. Or put another way, the demon demands a toll, a withholding tax, or quite possibly a severance, sin or death tax, for what maybe an eternal tax on the great pretender.

So, numb with whisky, or some other potent spirit, or with something else, maybe life in a niche, a bubble as a professional follower, yes-man, yes-woman, which can eventually seem quite weird, unreasonable, from all those scripts as well as roles that conflict and lack logic, yes, so especially numb a certain region of the brain, such as the aspect stuck in a loop, in a true obsession.

And better yet, quickly down a few potent drinks then utter a battle cry of freedom, "Let freedom ring!"

Or "Freedom reigns!"

And yes, use as a prop, a malaprop, support, proposition, and yet as if another proprietor, another boss or precarious substitute, of just another tenacious tether, another complex web or entanglement of a claustrophobic system, a trap, where any given system gives one freedom yet removes a few others, that technique, the technique of relief, of neutralization.

Regardless here and now, one group after another says to her, "We fully appreciate these new people and communities.

"It represents one of the most difficult processes, to add new people, the correct ones, and trait variety to add a fresh perspective, to create more than the sum.

"This place adds something special, such as a fresh breeze, new ideas, energy, abilities and places, beyond their normal annual migration route, beyond the traditional pattern of the World Economic Forum, Milken Institute Global conference, Allen & Company conference, TED, Super Bowl, Masters Golf Tournament, Wimbledon, Monaco Grand Prix, Concours d'Elegance, Royal Ascot, Triple Crown, and the four fashion world capitals of Milan, Paris, New York, and London, as well as Portugal, Rome, São Paulo, and Berlin and the food as well as wine festival migration, which includes Aspen, South Beach, San Diego, White Truffle and other premier events, and with an ever so brief stop at the Cannes Film Festival then devote far more time at Cannes Lions International Festival of Creativity.

"Yes, and less jet traffic, especially private jets, and where to park, close to these events, as things clutter.

"Yes, and avoid dreary Foggy Bottom meetings, with so many needy politicians, such as the professional panderer and just another cult, an *argumentum ad hominem*, based on a stale script, a logical fallacy, a dusty creed that uses an ever so shallow language game, such as a stale process, so avoid that modern version of Dante's *Divina Commedia*?

Of which Mary duly notes, yet reveals nothing of major consequence, or the fact she could not possibly take credit for any of these mansion events, or the fact she may be the great pretender.

Then at a significant conversation pause, a major branch, a decision tree, she steps away and into a group of professional ostrich babysitters, a group that specializes in difficult birds, quite.

And they explain in great detail about problematic birds, about birds who rarely satisfy ... and difficult people, at various ages, those transitions, and difficult couples, difficult pairs, yet more than a love interest, such as paired opposite, that dynamic of life in a quandary, a catch-22, Cornelian dilemma, no-win situation or Pyrrhic victory-based system.

So, a passenger tries to safely navigate within, such as avoid one wrong word, a script variation or tonal infraction, something not pitch-perfect, which the powers-that-be or social construct view as a serious slight, a serious offense, and because of the all-or-nothing-mechanism, the "all in or out tradition," often based on a whim or myth, which can trigger a major rollback event then removal of insider privilege, a rollback of exceptions, because you are not one of them, not pure. As a system, proxy, or mob might polarize and form, because of the smallest thing, often based on a factoid or rumor, as well as trivia, and very much so, as if much of any given system represents a trivial pursuit with exceptionally dangerous consequences based on minutia, for a small inflection error, from a blink at the wrong time, or failure to cheer loud enough at each slogan of the day, or on cue, on the mark.

And it often seems quite dangerous to say a small freedom of expression, and it reveals the obsessiveness many systems expect, and yet they often say "*locutions de minimis non curat praetor or de minimis non curat lex,*" that paired opposite, or preference for a meticulously selected paired opposites, dynamics, companions and the dependents of yet another trap, and why so many traps, why so many excuses to step on an ant, and really mash it. Or systematically eliminate the competition, the others, and not see them as part of the great quintessential stack, the supreme bulkhead, the totality of the universe, whether extinct or current, as if localized solutions to complex algebraic bubble yet string, and not sees them as part of the garden, the farm system: that great dilemma, such as a weed might ultimately represent a great sustainable opportunity, a founding system or frame, a manifold, topological space or community.

And regarding these ostrich specialists, these people seem to know far more than they will admit, especially about Mary, Maryport Shelby Segedunum, yet everyone simply calls her Mary, which as strange as it might seem, was born under a willow tree that stood next to a stone wall.

More importantly, people often best describe her as a "hello nurse," a natural brunette bombshell who focuses on a doctorate of nursing studies, and everything about her screams "Schwiiinnng!" as in stunning to the nth degree, and a classic beauty. So much so, it causes men and women an initial jolt to their senses, which discombobulates them in a distinct series of profound events.

However, her dress, manner, and movement deliberately understated attractiveness, as if to disguise it with every possible trick.

In addition, her efforts attempt to systematically conceal any trace of wow.

And most people have a first impression skill set, and some more than other. However, she is not able to fool that level of detection. Likewise, her methods consistently miss the mark, and seem off, yet in a way that comes across as clumsy, quite noticeable, and with a distinct lack of skill, which ultimately translates into a signature look, regardless of each newly created style to hide, and each new style appears as if a great effort.

Strangely enough, and after observing her for some time, something triggers within the observer, and it might connect to the adaptive unconscious, intuition, *déjà vu*, reason, or the under or oversoul, to the set, the setting, as well as context, and ignoring the fundamental rules of nature, system, symmetry or some combination.

Then each time, a series of mental events appear on the observer's face, distinct stages, which resemble elaborate measurements, formulations then a last-second resolution jolts to the same conclusion, and those mental events or moods transition from surprise, puzzle, engross, eager to move closer, hesitant, uneasy and cautious; then everyone goes out of the way to avoid Mary's secret.

The net result generates a powerful distancing effect, a field, such as if an exedra aspect of a subconscious conversation pit, or shared state, or ontic wave binding event that tags nearby things in memory, time and space, or as if a special workspace, not a psionic event, although it has a delta wave feel, a powerful ever so slow wave.

And even if a person were to eventually stand in her personal space. So much so, it creates an elephant-in-the-room effect, no one wants to mention the subject, so they honor her secret, and empiricism of art, the art of concealment.

Yet here and now they treat her as a long lost friend.

Moments later the dog arrives, which Mary fails to see, and it studies in great detail, especially a considerable number of mansion regulars, people who often arrive well after she departs for the weekend.

Then Mary enters the long hallway and meets another group who, oddly enough, write fortune cookies, "yes, for a living," as it represents a certain industry, well, as "a specialist, in a niche."

Beyond those writers stand whisky ambassadors, truly well-known industry experts, who, yes, dresses up as the British philosopher Jeremy Bentham at various stages of life, and they offer one poignant toast of honor after another as well as to her, and with exceptional wit, in fact quite remarkable, of memorable quotes with zip, with zing.

However with each saying, she slightly shrugs shoulders, or offers a specialized look each time, a special adjustment, of *sprezzatura*, a certain nonchalance, well, to conceal all art, all vital thoughts and mission regardless of each situation, which will give the full appearance of effortless and without telling thoughts, such a poker tell, and "Really?"

Yet she eventually hints at a considerable interest, with a wit construction, about life; however she does so with the minimum tell, yet quite visible to the group, the whisky ambassadors, true industry experts, and the very best. And as they all sip a rare whisky of peated malt, a thousand-year development or more, a bog or mire at the minimum, maybe a sphagnum or what, and smoked over burning peat, which imparts aroma and flavor, imparts characteristics, traits or notes. And yes, as it might eventually create a masterpiece, a single special malt, and with sufficient pure spirit in simple distillation stages, to make a cleaner and lighter spirit, of two-wash, four spirits, such as wash, feint, spirit, fore shot, dud run, wee witchee, and heart.

The water, was it from Rowan Tree Burn, the Scurran Burn and the Benrinnes Spring?

Regardless, the twenty-four-year-old whisky has considerable gravitas, a flavor threshold, with sophistication, such as a masterpiece, and what one expects at an elite event, such as the Pebble Beach *Concours d'Elegance*.

Then several groups of rock stars invite Mary, so she arrives, and their groupies maintain various distinct orbits, quite distinct, and all the while listen and wait for the slightest cue to admire, flatter, cherish and defend.

Another nearby group orbits a person, and they prop up this false star, prop up someone mistaken for the famous, because the style or tradition. And they operate full time, not as puppeteers, more so as if enablers for a person with very poor social skills, a person who easily offends, and the ground support team nervously monitors each and every word then justifies, then other members work as fantasy brokers, a support group to sell these ideas, this way of thinking to other professional grumps, such as loud and difficult to satisfy people.

And as Mary walks by hedge fund managers, they lament about how people portray them, as misunderstood and undertaxed, such as nobody fully understands their plight or burden, well, no sympathy as they sip *Chateau Cheval Blanc* 1947, *Romanée Conti* 1945, *Pétrus* Vintage 1961, while another nurses a fifty-year *Glenfarclas* and Chivas Regal Royal Salute; however another person chugs one bottle after another of SAPPORO Space Barley beer, while most of them drink spring water.

So they do what only seems best, a heated debate within reason, given the social circumstances, on whether to eliminate the capital gains as well as estates tax, and on cue a politician arrives.

Whereas Mary politely listens and when a natural lull arrives, one longer than normal, the type that indicates a major break or new branch, one that signals the group may completely change topics or break up and go their separate ways, she asks them, "Has anyone seen the hostess, the mansion owner?"

# Chapter

And most of them awkwardly react then sip a considerable amount of whisky or something else, with the hope it seeps into body, mind, and soul, into the incorporeal and immortal aspect if possible, and especially seep into the *psyche*, well, to create an equilibrium refinement, and vapor recovery quality, recovery from life, from so many complex situations, such as a vast number of problematic situations along the journey through life, to recover from one cult after another, to find original state as well as intent, what they were supposed to be in the beginning, that clarity with each sip, or at least numb the trouble tree, numb memories and the mental microbiome, the community of commensal, symbiotic and pathogenic microorganisms that share the mind, such as numb the citizens and illegal immigrants.

Yet eventually they hem, haw then question and explain as Mary listens for a considerable amount of time, "Does she ever show up?"

"Never."

"She's busy, quite."

And a few of them seem genuinely irritated, put off as if obvious, and one of them says, "No one sees the commander."

"She has no interest in the frivolous."

"Yes."

"I agree."

And others nod in full support of that statement.

"Much of her time is spent traveling."

"And no one knows much about her," which the group agrees as well as nearby groups, who lean towards and nod in full agreement.

"I know her," says a hedge fund manager, who stares at his glass of whisky served neat.

And heads turn.

This man appears late sixties, stocky, fit, and has a rugged face, solid Roman nose, and short mostly grey Caesar haircut.

Yet his last name is fforléans, no capital first letter, as the French Revolution compelled many to chop a name, and people pronounce it Fah-orléans, the family considered ffolliott, well, to appear ordinary and not *fils* de France, eventually they chose fforléans.

He started in the financial industry as a specialist in stochastic calculus and discrete markets, yet now works exclusively in the dark liquidity markets, looking for a mystery, a straw, such as behind a straw buyer.

"Yes, I know her.

"She was a Naval commander of an Arleigh Burke class guided missile destroyer (DDGs), the United States Navy's first class destroyer, one of the most powerful surface combat ships ever put to sea, and built around the Aegis Combat System, armed with Harpoon missiles, as well as nuclear warhead-tipped tomahawk missiles with a 1,550-mile range."

More people perk and edge closer.

"The Naval commander—she's a no-nonsense cuss master virtuoso.

"She can cuss with the best of them," then he sips whisky, which seeps into body, mind, and soul, into the incorporeal and immortal aspect if possible, and especially seep into the psyche, well, to create an equilibrium refinement, and vapor recovery quality.

Then he nods then exits for a refill, for a twenty-five-year-old whisky, a rare spirit, of peated malt, a thousand-year development or more, from a bog or mire, maybe a sphagnum or what, and smoke over burning peat, which imparts the character of a masterpiece.

And during his exit, rock star groupies locate him, locate opportunity, and turn on the charm, the magic, yet he barely rolls his eyes and instead reaches for something reliable, something ever so true, another glass of Glenfarclas, neat.

Meanwhile, Mary quietly slips away and moves past a group of quantum, subspace and temporal mechanics in a heated debate, a major philosophical debate, and they point toward the Proving Grounds.

And as she walks forward, yet looks back, she bumps into another group, a collection of FBI, CIA, NSA and DIA agents as well as their foreign counterparts in a huddle, leaning slightly into a tight semicircle, and each sips a high-octane drink, a potent concoction, such as a travel circuit special, to seep into the *psyche*, the vapor well, to recovery from life, from so many complex situations, and so many bad options, such as a vast number of problematic situations, and most made so by one restless industry or system after another, which rarely satisfy for more than a few moments, and a few agents worry, about unemployed, bankruptcy, homeless, a profound resume gap, a string bad relationships, as well as systematically alienated from family and friends, such as I've become the other, the underclass, that risk, one of those trapped in a system designed by and for the haves. Moreover the fact that most people do not fully realize the seismic shift underway, from a historic employment crisis in the United States of America and especially around the world, realize the major tectonic shift and profound k-wave of disruption, as well as the potential of a lost generation or two, well, until it affects them, which is often too late and leaves not enough time to adjust before the sudden impact.

Regardless of all that, as well as here and now at the gathering, each agent flashes a warm smile, extends a handshake and formally greeting to one another, which seems quite cordial, at least until you notice all the subtle clues of an interagency rivalry, yes, mano-a-mano or someone coveting someone else's stuff.

Regardless, these clues often appear and the mood grows tense, well, as the conversation laces with sarcasm, satire, cynical disregard, and caustic wit, an agency inside ....

As a result, and at the proper time, Mary slowly backs away and moves from room to room, Music, Ladies' Reception, Great Hall, and eventually up that main red carpet staircase, pass Flemish tapestries and elegant murals.

All the while, with a dispassionately look in each exclusive event, while studying the situation, and eventually each person from head-to-toe, especially the face, outfit, posture, gesture, idiosyncrasy, as well as motive, mood, tone, theme, orbit and other nuance.

Then outside the mansion, the long-lost mother of Bonnie, a woman named Bruno, arrives.

And, that portly fellow named Sauvignon notices, the person who seems a bit disheveled, in an ill-fitting outfit as well as role, as a style guide, a guide open source higher-order function—no, wait, a special reference desk guide, or reference library, a Zen survivor, visionary, truth-telling sage, yet good shepherd as well as wasteland elder.

And he motions to her with subtle head movement, down the road, and beyond those gates, go and see, see what they have done, yes.

Just as importantly, she seems the opposite of a helpless free woman, and she has the look as well as reputation of someone capable of a good fistfight, a transformative event, of no-nonsense, such as you have my full attention. So people offer her plenty of room, as she moves through that road, gates, mansion main doors and one group after another, of FBI, CIA, NSA and DIA agents in a huddle, hedge fund managers, venture capitalists, whisky ambassadors dressed up as the British philosopher Jeremy Bentham, elite patricians, socialites, tastemakers, as well as that transformative star-making system, the studio system in process then she passes a few superstars, divas, prima donnas, divos, primo uomo all-stars with a grand on- and off-stage personality, with style, with an ever so special flair, yet they offer her plenty of room to pass through, even the rock stars groupies.

All make way for Bruno, a fistic, and whose well-chronicled rise at a young age into the sport of bare-knuckle boxing, similar to the movie *Knuckle*, a film about the secretive world of Irish traveler bare-knuckle fights, as her mother lived in that closed world of the Irish travelers, and considered herself Irish, a Didicoy, a term for a mixed Romani and a non-Romani parentage child. And in her case it consists of a well-known Basque family with a reputation for more than a few ambitious, smart, rough and tumble rascals, especially the women. Yet the thick accent has long gone, however on occasion the mother curses in an Irish Travelers' dialect of Gammon and Cant.

And professional ostrich babysitters immediately nod respect, respect-for-the-ages, because they know human nature, and why risk losing ten years of life—just like that, gone, as the shock would denigrate personal reserves or those ten years instantaneously leap away, and go wherever elusive things travel then eventually find a new home, maybe absorbed back into nature.

Moments later, that old-school motorcycle officer appears; the one from a previous investigation. And before, he arrived on an old-school motorcycle, and fully clad in a pristine uniform, in fact spotless, one that resembles a uniform worn by the Massachusetts Metropolitan Police, a dark-colored outfit popular during the 1950s with jacket, as well as those special old-school pants with extra room in the upper thighs and hips, and the officer wears black leather gauntlet gloves, immaculate black leather boots, cap, and dark sunglasses.

And before, a whiff of something arrived—as it has the distinct hint of well-maintained leather, and the boots had a brilliant shine, which hint of polish, and not some ordinary version, not based on petroleum, alcohol, resin and silicone, yet one immediately recognizable as bee, carnauba and other vegetable waxes, along with mink-oil, pine, and a slight hint of something else, mineral—yes, the type used by a true professional—and all of which has been buffered into a transparent finish, with remarkable clarity that creates an unparalleled brilliant high-gloss shine. It may well be *Saphir Renovateur Medaille d'Or* Cleaner and Conditioner, as well as *Saphir Medaille d'Or Pate de Luxe* Wax Polish.

In addition and before, the officer stood with a stellar no-nonsense bearing, which seemed smart, fit, powerful and ready, ready for anything, and ready everything, as in that aspirational saying, "One Riot, One Ranger." And the way it should be in life, instead of an overwhelming team of local police or a Special Force commando team, as you most often need just one well-respected officer, whose name precedes arrival, and often that person goes by one name, or one classic phrase, and who reflects true greatness, seems dispassionate, as well as exceptional under tremendous pressure, which operates as coolant in full accord with nature, and some people might describe with the word "equanimity," as if in full accord with time and space, a mindful person in the here and now, and not struggling with mental phantasms, with baggage, yet a person who has fully educated personal demons with facts, with a full spectrum of knowledge, realism, perspective, and deploys a complex adaptive system, as well as a person who is the very foundation of democracy, equality, justice, freedom and especially humanity, and not a servant of the few: "One Riot, One Ranger!"

Regardless of all that, as well as here and now, and when the officer speaks, it shows command-and-control, and not command and conquer.

Also, the actions seem methodical, precise, and show true gravitas.

In that last mansion visit, the officer investigated something, a grotto, allegory of the cave, AB hylomorphs, Franz Kafka notions, Schröder–Bernstein theorem of measurable space, indexicality, as well as human aspects, and not in a conventional sense of the body, mind and soul, such as something you might find near the Well of Souls and that phase transition of things not easily quantifiable.

In addition, questions focused on broken windshield glass, a mangled mountain guardrail and damage to someone's classic red barn, as well as chicken coop. Apparently the chickens refuse to lay eggs, and as a result someone must pay for all that damage, and especially for the borrowed scenery, borrowed heap of opportunity now lost, for that leap, as well as an identity now in full crisis.

And of equal importance as well as here and now regarding the officer, he wears civilian clothing, in fact an impeccably tailored suit made with the finest materials, as if a true classic, and there appears something perfect about the officer—too precise, too superclean, and far beyond perfection.

Maybe you have seen those types of people, things, or situations; too perfect, such as perfect-pitch, perfect-fifth, or a perfect ten, citizen, couple, system, or the universal constitution, or universal wave function of theatrical property, and not a founding myth.

Also, the officer appears sublime, as if a living work of art, as one might describe with the Greek word *statikos*, and how James Joyce often used the words "proper art" to describe when some person, place, or thing had a look that invokes a state of esthetic arrest—as a viewer has neither the urge to move towards nor away from that object, but instead appears transfixed or arrested by the sight.

That seems an odd description, because "sublime" usually refers to sweeping vistas, majestic mountains, or some special combination, as well as exceptional view of land, sea, air and the heavens, of nature viewed with a remarkable amount of content, as well as context. Or, it usually refers to other extraordinary events, which also includes great misfortune, the tragic, for instance a carpet-bombing event, as a person must hide among the rubble of a home, village, town or city, and feel the full concussive power, and feel those series of tremendous impacts, and it produces an incredible sense of awe, disorientation, numbness, and reveals an unusually small self—in fact, a feeble being with marginal power, size and importance, a vulnerable being by design, and the personal bearings, as well as aurora of termination and bow shock, have been blasted away to reveal a true fragile core, such as a core-and-veneer-based dream cast wave system, and a self that must sit helpless among rubble, as yet another great war machine delivers full power, might and glory—it delivers the sublime.

Regardless, the officer discreetly confers with Bruno in great detail, about something, as if an update, and he points to one situation after another then offers to escort her about, such as to one of the operas, which includes Don Giovanni, *Orphée aux enfers*, *Dafne*, *Aida*, *The Marriage of Figaro* in full licentiousness form, as well as a Theatre of India play, a condensed version of Nalacharitham, Kathakali, a ritualistic love story drama, one of classical theatre forms of India with elaborate as well as colorful makeup, costumes, and face masks.

The latter is an ancient Kuttiyattam, a Sanskrit theatre of unknown origin with the traditional themes of folk mythologies, religious legends and spiritual ideas from the Hindu epics and Puranas.

In which the actors show distinct eye, hand, and foot movements, with precision, especially the mannerisms, communication techniques and martial arts, which seem quite unusual, as if some other system of thought, or originated on some other world, or once the aliens arrived, they communicated this way, or this was their opera storytelling system, or one more likely humans might understand, more relatable, relevant, and with movements as if living art.

And that Nalacharitham is scheduled to start within moments, a condensed version of, which she shows a minor interest then attends.

Of which, Bruno arrives and word spreads to people in various events, which include Gus, Livia, Mero, that German patrician, Chris Overbeck and previous homeowner, which causes a minor commotion, as their eyes narrow.

In fact, in each room, nearly everyone is period-correct with costumes, manner and speech, except for an occasional redneck, manga counterculture style of pre-WWI Greece, Stilyaga, Gopnik, member of the lost generation, hipster, and a few redshirts.

And eventually those vital people arrive at the Nalacharitham play, survey all guests in great detail then enter after Livia dressed as Marie de' Medici, Mero as Averardo de' Medici, and a scientist dressed as Francesco I de' Medici.

Moments later Albizzi and Strozzi arrive.

As all this takes place, someone peeks through the India play curtain and fixates on one of the new arrivals, then replaces the story with vital sections of Mahabharata, an epic narrative of the Kurukshetra War, a story about the fate of struggling dynastics, of too-big-to-fail, and written in the Gupta Empire during the Golden Age of India.

Then one by one, as the actors move through a secret as well as narrow mansion passageway then someone or thing removes them, until only the lead actor remains, the type of person who talks and talks as members listen, well, begrudgingly they must.

And it resembles a long soliloquy of personal experience, quite, the type that causes people to cringe, as those things seem too personal, yet some people lack a filter or they are the boss, and the worker must listen as well as love or else.

Regardless, and eventually, all replacement actors or things emerge through the curtains, which the dog carefully studies in great detail, then exits to the library, to see if anyone has moved books, especially the first three shelves, and no interest in the two shelves above, other books, a reserve, reserve-of-sparks, of tried and true classics with occasional mention of the golden rules, especially of caution, maybe as an understudy, a reserve, maybe a quintessential, that bookshelf of reserves, which study the vitals, such as the subconscious, self-reference, perspective, imagination, atonement, and connection to the under as well as oversoul.

And yes, someone removed a few books on various shelves and added others, as each book as well as placement matters; it really matters, especially regarding a sequence dependency, or a dependency-based parse tree, which the dog immediately notices, as well as the abstract placement pattern, ever so complex, and that greater message, as well as the thematics, that pattern of.

# CHAPTER 25

In the meantime, Mary closely observes other things, as these events grew more and more elaborate, such as world-class bands, and exotic event themes become the norm.

In fact the buzz traveled great distances, to the far corners of the country and beyond, along with a very strict timetable, rules and who might attend, which developed into an ever so exclusive list.

And each time the events shut down well ahead of schedule, well before early Sunday morning, which allows more than enough time to clean, restore, and move traffic.

Just as importantly, most people work as a team to put everything back in place, and did so quite civil, which seems remarkable, and they rely on a detailed set of-before-photographs mounted in an ever so thick set of three ring binders, to insure everything returns to the exact place.

And normally Mary would arrive on Sunday late morning, and things had already fully restored well before that, plus everyone had departed except the designated babysitter, who patiently waits with a beaming smile, as a full spectrum of course, well according to the theory, and done so to not raise concerns, not seem too happy, as well as too satisfied. Because most people rarely achieve that in a given day, a full spectrum, such as elate and enthusiastic, that mode of discovery, which represents something a person might experience in a gold rush, with someone who has found a truly great fortune, a California dream or the Klondike, Australia, New Zealand, South Africa, South America, such as Brazilian gold rush and the *Tierra del Fuego* gold rush, so hide that look?

And things seemed to go well, in fact excellent for the ultimate event and partygoers.

Yet here and now Mary finds no event planner, no person in that role, no one in charge of the overall process, no central planning, as it seems to self-organize, to have a life of its own, such as ownerless property, or psychology ownership compared to legal ownership, that type of organizational behavior, of behavioral clustering at different levels, or superimposition, temporal stub, and sunken kingdom to reemerge.

Again today represented an exception, as Mary returned early.

And of considerable note, someone is pregnant, yes, so rumors fly, and news swirls at the mansion as people whisper.

So much so, a huge upstairs hillbilly Appalachia hoedown approaches to a complete stop, and yet the dance caller continues to say, "Allemande left and Do-se-do," until realizing everyone has long stopped.

Then Tommy, yes Tommy, who joined an event eventually motions for the musicians to lay down their instruments, which includes fiddle, bass, guitar, washboard and others things, as people look about.

And of equal importance, Tommy wants to know who is pregnant. "Please step forward?"

Regardless, the room remains silent.

In fact, no one moves.

So she says, "OK, just raise your hand, wink, or nod.

"Give an ever so subtle hint.

"Give us a sign, so we can get back to the hillbilly Appalachia hoedown.

"Come on, man up."

Yet no one comes forward.

And Mary remains hidden, to carefully study all aspects, which might reveal the entire mansion story.

And she does so as Tommy moves through the crowd, and closely looks at each hillbilly from head to toe, looks for any sign.

"Hey, what's so difficult about admitting you're pregnant?

"Are you afraid of something?

"Got something to hide?"

And no one answers.

So she continues moving among the crowd of upscale hillbilly and carefully looks at each person, as well as their outfit from head to toe then eventually arrives at Emma and notices a glow, a real glow, radiance.

"Emma."

And the crowd surges towards them.

Then Tommy notices even more, "Samantha.

"And Reece?"

The crowd shocks, and a few jaws drop, as well as "Oh my!" because it seems absolutely clear all three are pregnant, and all three radiate beyond description, as well as being indeed.

# CHAPTER

Then Benny slowly raises her hand and the party crowd stands absolutely shocked, as all four pregnant close friends edge closer to one another, and closer.

Then a large circle forms around them, as people ask who, what, where, when, how and other questions.

Yet these ladies say nothing.

And they offer no clues whatsoever, none.

Then these upscale hillbillies whisper and wonder.

Some scratch their heads.

Most gawk.

A few shrug.

Moments later, a very upset Tommy wedges her way through the crowd and moves towards the center, then waves her arms to gather everyone's attention and says, "Okay, okay, okay.

"First of all, I'm absolutely shocked, totally, and I had no idea.

"Well, because people keep me out of the loop, which really offends me.

"I'm offended.

"I'm upset.

"I thought we were friends.

"And yet, I … well," she pauses, looks about to carefully consider, to be discreet, okay, more discreet than normal, yet her real focus turns inward, looking in various places for something, anything, maybe a well-turned phrase, or crude curse or a sharp wit to sting.

Instead, a spark catches her and turns into a serious disappointment yet eventually a smile.

Then she decides to continue speaking and intently looks at each and every one, yet something changes, really changes, and she replies as if a hillbilly and says, "Ima thankin, as close as I can figger, we can stand here and cumplain'n aboit, makin a big deal, pointin fingers and astin lots of private questions, such as who, whut, whar, whatever, whut mighta been or we can support our friends.

"So, we don't need no xplainayshun.

"Listen up, I have a solushun.

"Let me pallgize.

"We need to count our blessins.

"It's an honor and eggcitin to become an auntie.

"I promiss to be an excellent one, hepful, luvin, one who respecks your wishes.

"Yessiree, this calls for a celebratin, a hillbilly celebratin," then Tommy carefully looks at each crowd member.

"Who's with me."

They tepidly agree.

Tommy roars, "I said, who's with me?"

And the crowd loudly roars an approval.

Then with a robust effort, the fiddlers ignite a genuine hillbilly Appalachia hoedown, which the crowd stomps to the beat.

# CHAPTER 27

Not much later, Mary secretly exits into the hallway, and not soon after, Benny, Emma, Tommy, Reece, Samantha, Vera, Mel, Zoey, Quinn and Seska converge from several directions.

Of which, Mary notices, steps into the shadows and carefully listens, as all of these ladies rush, meet, fret and warn of impending doom, because reports arrive that Mary roams the mansion, and has meticulously investigated event activity as well as the history of.

And with all of that uproar and buzz from various celebrations, concerts, groups and subgroups, the ladies have to speak quite loud, to hear each other.

However, all these various events under one roof reach a lull at the same time, a natural pause of quiet, well, before the next segment or branch begins, if any.

And call it fate, justice, the natural order, bad luck, bad choice, poor timing, the randomness of nature, or thrownness of nature, thrown into life, and a world with millions and millions of rules, laws, regulations, decrees, norms, expectations and axioms, most unwritten, and it seems impossible to know even a fraction of them, and yet a person must obey all at the same moment, obey this very complex gnarl of contradictions.

The gal pals' voices boom a summary about Mary, her bad habits, especially all that clutter, such as digs through nursing school supplies, furiously rummages pass books, lab materials, overdue bills, wrinkled and tattered notes, school garments, outfits, a lost class schedule, and project procrastinations, and particularly her poor judgment of secretly outsourcing of babysitting duties to Benny, Emma, Tommy, Reece, and Samantha, yes, Samantha, Vera, Mel, Zoey, Quinn and apparently Seska, as well a host of strangers, such as ostrich babysitters.

And during the event lull, their voices travel a great distance.

So much so, the crowds notice then group after group turns toward them, as Mary appears, which seems quite clear she overheard everything and shows an evil eye, a malevolent glare, which, if possible, would serve as a death ray, a beam of destruction to incinerate things, to crisp things, or melt steel on contact, or create eternal smolder.

Of which, the gal pals fully realize and want to flee, to scram, to exit stage left.

So much so, the body of each repeatedly starts and stops in fits, on where to jump or run, and especially with an impulse to leap, maybe leap out a window, and a fast exit to some distant place. Maybe they can eventually settle on an uninhabited tropical island, with a single coconut tree, or settle in a remote Tibetan mountain cave, used by a wild-haired and crazy-eyed guru, who often spouts cryptic sayings about life, about how to live in such a weird system, a system of so many contradictions, and "bunga-bunga."

Or flee to Socotra Island—one of the most alien, bizarre, and desolate places on Earth, or escape to Pitcairn Island and console among the few remaining direct descendants of the HMS Bounty who original wanted a reasonable naval alternative, a reasonable life, reasonable water, food, accommodations, and culture as well as an occasional lime or substitute, a well-established known.

Regardless, the gal pals consider a window escape, at same time, and they would settle for a quiet shimmy out, that tight squeeze of everyone at the same time, that struggle.

Moments later, and in the room below, where the comatose man lies, a loud noise bangs, "Hmm!" and a loud commotion, then rapid sounds, "Tmp, tmp, tmp, tmp, tmp!" on the hardwood floor, as well as a loud thud and more rapid sounds, "Tmp, tmp, tmp, tmp, tmp!" on that same dark Brazilian cherrywood floor.

As a result, Mary leaps through the gal pal meeting, nearly stumbles down that main red carpet staircase, pass Flemish tapestries and elegant murals enters the room, and finds eight men, massive brutes who have a professional all-pro-football-player look, superfit with muscles stacked on muscles, all well over six-foot four, 275 pounds and above, dressed as Bette Davis, Dorothy from the Wizard of Oz with sparkling ruby slippers, Xena the Warrior Princess, Gabrielle, Marlene Dietrich, Mae West, Cher the Goddess of Pop and Tammy Faye, yet the creepy versions, quite, and not on purpose, from so many poor fashion decisions.

Regardless, Mary snaps and sees red, as all that fascination and dispassionate curiosity vanishes.

The feral arrives, which causes her to boil then her mind adjusts with the face showing clear steps of deliberate thought, and she eventually says, "Who put you up to this, Ray Lewis, Matt Damon, Ben Affleck, Brad Pitt, George Clooney?"

No reply.

Then with a commanding voice wholly out of character, she says, "Regardless, there are going to be a few fistfights.

"Line up and take your beating like a man."

And after considerable thought by the players, then a series of rock-paper-scissors, they eagerly line up in a specific order, Tammy Faye, Gabrielle, Bette Davis, Xena the Warrior Princess, Dorothy from the Wizard of Oz with sparkling ruby slippers, Cher the Goddess of Pop, Marlene Dietrich, and Mae West.

Yet apparently they do not move fast enough, so she says to the biggest and meanest one, the one with a ferocious scowl and wildly insane look, and who stands six-foot eight, weighs 320 pounds and dresses as Dorothy from the Wizard of Oz, "I'm going to grab Tammy Faye by the ankles then use her to beat you unconscious."

Then he or she pushes buddies aside and makes to the front line.

And he or she says, "I'm gonna give you a choice—a good old-fashioned fistfight or a curbside stomp."

"Any way you wanted, girly man," Mary says, and they fight.

# CHAPTER 28

Elsewhere, and the next morning in a deep sleep, on that small wooden bed, which might remind a person of *Forrest Bed, The Architect's Brother*, yet of peony shrubs and something else, Bonnie slowly revives then shifts about.

Her mind tries to focus, and moments later gain a forest orientation, as well as the irresistible impulse to immediately turn her attention north, towards the nearest mansion property marker, and that persistent feeling then becomes all-consuming.

Everything else fades, becomes pale, even the all-powerful Moon Pie, and her focus narrows even more as the face takes on a serious, determined, and steady look.

Unable to move beyond these thoughts, she rises from the bed, stretches, dons the meticulously cleaned backpack and struggles through dense vegetation toward that first property marker, as the dog launches into the lead, which causes her to sizzle from its persistence, and not willing to go away: be gone, and the fact it uses a point-to-this-and-that-method then takes a circuitous route, a complex one with few straight line.

As a result she eventually grumbles and ignores, then without knowing steps pass one trip wire and sensor after another until the dog issues a few quiet woofs then points true, steady, and motionless at each one.

Of which, she shrugs it off and takes one shortcut after another, which seem a bit less time-consuming yet they still require a complex path through thick tangled growth, especially thickets, a path with few straight lines, plenty of dangerous thorns, many pauses, even requiring frequent belly crawls, as struggle, strain, stretch, contort, climb and squeeze between narrow obstacles.

After two hours, something snaps ahead, maybe a dry twig.

So she freezes.

Then more sounds arrive from that same direction, "fshht," which come in four groups of three.

Seconds later, several things thud, then drag.

And silence arrives.

Eventually a wild-eyed Special Forces soldier desperately crawls from that direction, and once reaching cover, he rises and quietly runs through the bewildering maze and away from the sublime towards safety through wait-a-minute-shrubs, and all the while straining to gain maximum distance.

This heavily armed commando collides into her then says with a thick foreign accent, "What the...?"

And his face transitions from overwhelmed and anxious to surprise, then suspicious, smug, mischievous, greed, then lust.

As a result Bonnie speechlessly backs away.

Then his confidence immediately returns, quickly shifting from prey to something else, as he looks at her from head to toe, and at her shape, especially each and every curve, as well as the complexion, which represents a look women know all too well.

Of which she instantly chills and feels discomfort.

Then the commando closely inspects her from various angles and says with hint of a greedy cruel smirk, "I'm trying to remember the exact term.

"The term they use to describe you—'a drifter.'

"I remember, they said a '*waif*' lives among the sticks, a '*guaif*,' a stray, 'a helpless frail wisp' far removed from society," then says slowly as well as ever so sly, "yes, a forsaken, homeless, and a redshirt."

Then he adjusts the weapon silencer, which seems unlike any known example, and decades ahead, "I see.

"This place will crush you, destroy your soul.

"Are you here to shout at the devil?"

And this causes her to stand speechless, and each attempt to speak generates lip movement, yet no sounds.

Then he offers a direct warning, about going to that plot of land, north, the property map reference, "If you go, you will die.

"Everyone who goes there dies!

"Everyone."

Then the soldier carefully measures her curves then innocence, and he edges forward into personal space as well as studies each remarkable curve.

Of which she edges backward.

And he says, "This is an unforgiving place, sly, brilliant and wholly treacherous.

"The only people who enter this forest are pawns, disposable people.

"We are unimportant, the odds and ends.

"And few people will remember us once we are gone."

Then she continues to slowly back away, as he edges forward then stares in her eyes with a greedy look, and at each inviting curve of her body.

And without the slightest hint, a grisly American Special Forces combat veteran arrives, one ordered to watch these foreign forces during their mission.

Moments later, the wayward soldier immediately straightens then merges with a now seen squad of foreign commandos.

And this American is an old-school tough guy sergeant, a lifer, Bazooka Joe, no-nonsense, stocky, no neck, Roman nose and a gravel voice which all comes across as commanding, and a man who could easily fit in a 1950's film *noir* movie, as the hardboiled plainclothes detective, a seen-it-all person.

Then the veteran subtly motions to the team: direction, distance, and full set of other instructions.

Just as quickly, they disappear into the forest.

In another direction, at a distance, a twig snaps.

And Bonnie looks, yet sees nothing.

Then something lightly bounces off her head.

However with a look about, she sees nothing of note.

Again, something bounces off her head.

Looking in all directions, nothing.

Another pea-size rock lightly bounces off her crown, her temple, or said another way, the park, terrace, or temple prime.

And as she turns, one bounces off her forehead, the space a person might call the third, inner, mystical or esoteric eye.

And crouched in a dense ticket, the grisly American Special Forces combat veteran motions to her with minimum movement, to lower with stealth then ever so quietly crawl toward his position, and he does so with a special sign language, which seems quiet efficient.

Of which Bonnie considers, carefully lowers then edges toward him.

And once there, he places an index finger to his mouth indicating stealth, which causes a puzzle look on her face, then he slowly points to something.

However, she looks and looks, yet sees nothing of note.

So he motions to look very carefully.

And she looks among the thick foliage.

Eventually, something becomes clear, a meeting, and the veteran says with a matter-of-fact whisper, "The one in the middle is known among clandestine operations as the Punk Buster, the Trickster, the Glorified Mummer.

"He is not a creature of the CIA or other clandestine agencies, though the CIA did make the mistake of trying to recruit him once, and that proved an absolutely shocking lesson to the fossilized system, the bureaucracy.

"This forest is called The Proving Grounds, a vast unofficial nation-state within a nation-state, and yet as if an embassy with its own very particular set of rules. It is home of the original DARPA, home to one of the scariest freaks ever associated with the field of PSYOPS, psychological warfare.

"The thing is a specialist in asymmetrical clandestine warfare, phantom warfare whether boots on ground, as well as techno wizardry, such as cyber defense that includes anti-and retro-bot asymmetrical warfare.

"The Punk Buster wears an unconventional outer layer, a combat-ready system of dragon ballistic scales made with tunable and nonlinear metamaterials, which adjusts its radiant properties to absorb electromagnetic energy or project it with great precision, much as a cuttlefish can change color and light polarization to camouflage and communicate, such as a chromatophore.

"This device captures background light, the setting, the physical qualities, such as pattern, connections as well as systems, and actively matches."

Moments later, this creature or thing communicates in poetic yet cryptic languages, versions of *Dispilio*, Linear A, *Cascajal* Block, *Quipu*, *Rongorongo*.

Then it displays bizarre colors and patterns that roll, flash, and blip.

And this meeting includes some of the most bizarre characters, all wearing different and highly ritualized mask, even the animals wear masks.

And three members, who may well be people or creatures, wear something that might remind a person of a Nick Cave sound suit, a suit with attached things, such as tin toys and another has an eclectic assortment of attached everyday objects.

And each of these three moves in very peculiar ways, as if a high ritual, a scientific *symposia* yet *emic* and *etic,* as specialists.

All done as five angry grizzly bears eagerly listen for instructions, and thin streams of incense smoke rise from an ineffable living rocklike thing, which sits on an elaborate altar, and the smoke smells of Storax, frankincense, Indian hemp, thistle yet something is not quite right, is missing, and these smells fill the air then give a mystical illuminating effect, a glory.

All of this appears as if an elaborate ceremony, and with overtones of the seasonal death-rebirth ritual and the system of invention.

Of equal importance, this process and system has the look and sound of *religio*, yet not in a religious sense, related to the word origin, and long before religion and its institutions grew ever so complex, and before all that bureaucracy, those layers and layer of snarl, of entanglement that any given system develops over time, all that gridlock, as well as mission drift.

Here and now, all their activity points to that living boulder, at the center.

As a result Bonnie and the grisly combat veteran continue to study events then she shifts ever so slightly, to get a better vantage point, and all the while try to avoid kneeling on dry leaves and twigs that might crackle.

Eventually both observers become caught up and effected on a psychoactive level by these cryptic ancient language messages, bizarre colors, patterns, roll of images, flashes, blips, timings and smells, which produce a trance, an altered state of awareness or consciousness, such as what a person might experience with the ancient Delphi Oracle, a dazed semiconsciousness, another version of a sensible state, such as a crossover trial on the sixth hour, a trial-and-error conditioning yet a secular event.

Moments later, the event ends with a blip then unusual Elizabethan purple halo, an aureole of unknown origins, as if a poetic truth, a glory or gloriole, which marks the end then wisps of smoke dissipate.

After that, the Punk Buster speaks three words, and instead of a traditional voice, out blast three tremendous warnings, a cross between a fog horn and thunderous bass.

And with that the animated boulder returns to a solid state then descends underground.

Seconds later another light flashes and all members vanish.

Eventually, the grisly combat veteran stands, brushes off the uniform and says, "Okay, I can retire now—really seen it all.

"It's safe to stand. This immediate area will remain quiet for another eight minutes or so."

Then he transmits hand signal messages and that combat team arrives within a minute.

"I've got to go.

"My time is up," and the chiseled veteran looks intently at her. "Have you eaten?"

And she still seems thunderstruck by the series of events.

"Have you eaten?"

Bonnie remains speechless.

He orders, "Bring the box," and a commando delivers it to her, then the veteran motions a quick team exit, out of the forest before time expires, before the big hurt.

And they quickly disappear within rustling foliage which marks the departure.

Moments later, a smell arrives, which she quickly notices and looks about, as eyes widen.

"Holy smokes," then Bonnie rips open the box, and inside are two large pulled pork sandwiches, coleslaw and potato salad, all homemade, and underneath sit braised beef short ribs, twice-baked russet potatoes with sour cream, cheddar cheese, extra crispy bacon, sauté onions and butter, as well as a considerable amount of grilled corn-on-the-cob, of which the sight and smell cause her to drift into a delightful place, a savory world.

# CHAPTER 29

Elsewhere, Agrippa lands at a Deep South airport.
And in due course, she struggles with one bag after another, that classic airport trudge, a true struggle of frustration as well as grump, such as when will airport travel improve?

Eventually, she stuffs them into a subcompact rental car, and drives away while occasionally scanning a meticulous set of investigative notes in one hand and the other on the steering wheel, with a two-finger lap-high driving style in this unfamiliar place.

Not much later, the road signs says, *NEXT EXIT, NATCHEZ, MISSISSIPPI.*

Too late—she misses it because of that reading habit, and curses for the next few minutes, without repeating the same foul word, a skill learned from her rocky stint in the Navy, from that very quick climb up the ranks, as well as brief time as a Naval commander, Arleigh Burke-class guided missile destroyer, a United States Navy's first class destroyer built around the Aegis Combat System, with Harpoon and Tomahawk missiles, a true nuclear threat, a ship designed to deliver long range and exact punishment, as expressed by the phrase "the ability to deliver a first strike, and pulverize, as well as reduce something into smithereens, into atomic dust."

She represents a bold cuss master tradition among commanders, which continues to this day in military service, and warriors who curse above and beyond everyday foul mouth themes. In fact these tough cuss virtuosos exist; well, they thrive and deploy a high cultural style within this low-brow art form. Think of it as a sweet science of exceptional foulspeak, designed to shock and provoke the senses, and yet when done in a certain way, it can reveal a well-seasoned mind, certain refined judgment, sentiment and taste, even charm as well as scholarship—as odd as that sounds—with a well-crafted mastery of language especially aesthetics, of nature, art, beauty, taste, and the sublime.

Offshoots exist. And most have a long-standing tradition, such as a warrior poet, someone tough and courageous in battle, and yet has a certain cultured bearing, refinement and well-seasoned mind, the agile type—and more than capable of delivering a fistic lesson, or a spinning karate chop to the throat, and again, and again, or reveal some extraordinary scholastic insight, as well as contemplate the big questions of life, and the universe, as opposed to a savage, a barbarian, or common thug.

Though Agrippa has none of those poetic skills, she does qualify as a cuss master by necessity, and did so to survive. Because in the military system, women must make more than a few adjustments, compromises, and sometimes must use very crude tools as well as techniques associated with the primal male—to avoid showing any sign of weakness, avoid showing certain refined culture, which includes symbolic nicety tokens of consideration and other crucial elements of a truly civilized system, for example, a sense of compassion and mercy for the weak or victim, which represents two components of true greatness, two of those pesky things, so hide them.

Eventually, Natchez appears.

Then the car passes through one of the oldest and most important European settlements in the lower Mississippi River Valley.

It served as the Mississippi territorial capital and was previously home of wealthy Southern planters, quite, and who constructed many of the finest antebellum homes, such as places of exceptional style, elegance and charm.

However, in this area many people remain quite bitter and reactive to this day, especially about the American Civil War, civil rights and especially the handling of cold cases, of so many missing people, burned down property, and other truly tragic events from vigilante justice, and that ethos of raw emotions, the mob, of swift justice without a trial by juror of peers or interest in all the facts as well as full context, without prudence and virtue, or the nineteen primary Roman virtues, or a community that Jeremy Bentham might fully appreciate, might celebrate as well as honor, such as a Golden Age of Enlightenment, yet Southern style, in their own unique way, well, to reach their full potential, to become their version of a truly great society, as well as foundation of the greatest nation-state system ever, that elusive path.

However mission drift occurs, which can happen to any idea, person or system, and one conflict after another, such as against a social construct, maybe gender, family, tribe, team, politic, culture, race, economic system, religion or some other form of creed, that well-worn path, habit or addiction of a quick fix—the step-on-an-ant syndrome, step on a generation, style, idea, the others or a weed, for whatever reason, such as the business of pitting one group against another, that technique to frustrate, agitate and escalate to no end, as well as hypervigilant, and ready for another fight yet quite tired and a few paychecks from bankruptcy again, that vicious circle of decades, centuries as well as the history of human species, and they are often told by a system to keep digging in the quagmire.

After another close look at those notes, Agrippa turns off the main road, and within forty minutes the car enters "The Sticks" as that paved road narrows, and car hits one bone-jarring pothole after another, while houses go from well-managed to a state of disrepair, or a state associated with the inability to collective grief, and that long journey to the other side, other side of the pillow, or dream, or journey: escape, and journey into a better light, and not the light-headedness of the same-old, same-old.

And now and again, a couch rest on the front porch, along with an easy chair as well as sundries, and off to the side sit rusting abandoned vehicles, tires and miscellaneous stuff, which often represent unfinished projects, procrastinations, or thought of another way, in a more positive light, think of these piles as a personal hardware store, and in many cases several generations worth of material.

A closer look at one front porch couch shows extensive duct tape repair patches here and there.

Apparently in this world, duct tape has a universal and beloved appeal, and rightly so, as if it were considered one of the finest products ever invented, and able to repair a considerable number of things, such as plumbing pipes, toolboxes, bumpers and boat leaks, as well as reseal bags of snacks to maintain crunch, for instance cheese puffs, potato chips, pretzels, caramel popcorn and other classic snacks that include Twizzlers, Whoppers, Raisinets, Goobers, gummy bears, and Jujyfruits.

Just as importantly, a person can use this tape to construct a hammock, and one with a beer and fishing rod holder—so that person can relax and recover on a spectacular sunny day—well, after a bar fight, a fistic event, fist city, such when you lay a fist on someone, a few times, such as Bubba, Austin, Hunter, Billy, Bobby Joe, Buck or Cooter.

And hell, a person can make a duct tape boat then paddle to an even better fishing location, a secret place, and if need be, to open waters.

Moreover and once there, cast a fishing line in alligator-infested waters, where a person might eventually realize something else, something very important, duct tape removes arm hair, "Ouch!" and "Ouch!"

And will all that hair regrow, such as on the arm and chest?

Hell, if need be, a person could repair clothing, and heck, even make a prom outfit, or better yet, a car racing stripe—well, no, never mind.

Just as importantly as Agrippa drives, Confederate flags fly here and there to remind everyone that the war never ended.

It was a stalemate, and the South will eventually separate sooner or later, to form a new superpower, a world-class nation in its own right, and have an unparalleled ability to exert influence and project power on a global scale, the true test with an unparalleled throw-weight across vast distances, as well as into deep space, the deep vacuum of interstellar space, as well as intergalactic and extragalactic.

And of note, as well as maybe not on par with the last point, signs here and there proudly declare that *A GOOD OLD BOY'S BEST FRIEND IS DYNAMITE.*

Eventually she turns and enters an unpaved road, which produces a dirt cloud trail, and on either side bushes appear mostly as sticks with a bit of green.

Then the car passes one abandoned shack after another, many of which awkwardly lean.

And just after a junkyard, the car turns on another dirt road, then within two miles it arrives at a small factory, a pale blue prefab, where on the outside sits a dozen mud-laden pickup trucks and three cars.

Just as significantly, nearly every truck has a gun rack, as well as bumper stickers which include Confederate flags, and various bumper sticker, such as *I'M NOT RACIST, I'M JUST EDUCATED.*

*THE SOUTH WILL RISE AGAIN.*

*IMMIGRANTS – GET OUT.*

*SHOOT FIRST, ASK QUESTIONS LATER.*

*MOMMA'S PACKING HEAT.*

*YES, TRUCKERS DO OWN THE ROAD.*

And without interest or concern about any of that, just a keen focus on getting answers, Agrippa exits the rental car with a Massachusetts license plate, that type of luck then stretches here and there for a considerable amount of time, for relief, real relief, and really stretches in search of satisfaction.

So much so an arm reaches, trunk twists, and leg extends: for the best technique.

And what is the best technique after a long sit, a long drive through space, as if space-faring nation unto oneself, the untold story?

And what represents the best methods to find real relief, as well as satisfaction then mellow with a well-being glow?

How does a person find that position then glow, as well as generate a halo, an original glory, a nimbus that surrounds a person and radiates beams of everlasting virtue and majesty, an aureole of unknown origins, or poetic truth, or gloriole, which resembles a totality, or a restored state, and also when the mind and garment act as one? As they related to the classical abstract

Latin noun of *velificatio*, a certain billow effect from the breeze, and the way it was supposed to be in the beginning, with a swirl of new ideas, possibilities, events, expansions into that great mystery.

As, that state appears in art, the classics, especially during the Renaissance, Renaissance Humanism, Neoclassicism and the Age of Enlightenment, and the Romantic era version. Where, a person resembles truth, beauty and mysterious beam of completeness, of totality, a majestic glory, becomes a fully realized redemption, the source of a great culture, becomes the source of a truly great civilization, as well as a vapor, the atmospherics, and ethereal yet vivid universal dream of a psychonautic, that sails through distinguished states, properties, *sui generis*, especially the *qualia*.

So, stretch.

"Yes."

As, onlookers notice, as well as the license plate, then she walks pass a man who intently looks at her, and with a very direct stare into the eyes then he splits tobacco to the side, and in a way that leaves a bit that drips on the lower lip and chin, which he slowly wipes with a shirt sleeve, and does so while looking directly into her eyes.

Once inside the building people turn, look and eyes narrow then a bear of a man approaches wearing a t-shirt that says, *IF YOU SMILE, I'LL PUNCH YOU IN THE FACE*, and he chews something then looks as if measuring her from head to toe.

Of equal importance, nearly everyone seems armed, such as Glock, Ruger LCP, Smith & Wesson M&P Shield 9mm, Sig Sauer P229 9mm and Kahr CM9/PM9, and some wear a black tactical thigh-holstered pistol with a Y-harness leg straps, while others wear a black carbon fiber composite belt loop-holstered weapons with a speed cut, for a fast draw, well, maybe a terrorist might appear, or more likely an ex.

Or more likely, a family member disputes something, or ex-wife, ex-girlfriend, coworker or boss, yes.

Moments later, a bear of a man says bluntly, "What?"

And Agrippa says, "I need a suit."

Then the men seriously look at her and say nothing.

So, she repeats, "A suit."

And everyone looks as well as measures her from head to toe.

"I called yesterday."

No one replies.

Eventually, that bear of a man stops chewing and says in a thick Southern good-old-boy accent, "Massachusetts."

"What, I'm here to buy a suit?"

So, he continues, "You're from Massachusetts?"

Then with a puzzled, "No, I'm from New York."

A few men shake their heads no.

And he continues, "Do you know you where you are?"

She says, "In a factory trying to buy a suit."

"You're in the Deep South."

"Is Jimmy here? I talked to him on the phone yesterday about a custom-made suit."

Regardless he shows a critical frown, spits tobacco, and says "I'm Jimmy, and I know nutin' about a suit."

"I see.

"Jimmy makes custom suits, diving suits, underwater diving."

Of which, he looks at her as if she is weird, as well as annoying, and his eyes narrow, "Are you from the government?"

"No."

"The Feds?"

"No."

"From that maritime research agency, what's the name?"

"No."

"Okay, the factory is round back.

"Go out the front, then around back.

"Ask for Roscoe—nobody calls him Jimmy," and the other men chuckle and nod, "Jimmy—can you believe that?"

So she exits, goes around back, cannot seem to find anyone here or there.

Eventually, she hears something, follows and finds a guy tinkering with a dive suit.

So she says "Roscoe?"

Of which, it causes the man to sizzle, really sizzle as eyes bulge, transfix, and try to burn a hole in her, if possible, then he rushes to her ready to fight, a fistfight, a knockdown, drag-out fistfight.

As a result she pats the air, "Whoa!

"Wait a minute, I ... I....

"I don't know what's going on; I'm here for a diving suit."

So, he stops. "Nobody calls me Roscoe, ever."

"But.

"OK," then she peeks around the corner, towards the building front then mood shows a serious irritation, especially about that trick as first impression seems vital, to a fresh start and not same-old, same-old.

Yet eventually her mood softens into relief, relief she eventually found him, especially after that long circuitous route here.

In front of the building, the heavily armed men laugh as well as high-five, "Roscoe."

In back of the building, she says, "My fault.

"I've called about the diving suit."

Then he eventually settles and says, "Yes, yes, we build and repurpose all types of diving systems, including diving suits or ADS, atmospheric diving suits" then invites her inside a tightly packed workspace, which does not look like an advanced manufacturing plant, not fancy, not leading edge, not a world-class manufacturer, or part of a world-class advanced manufacturing center, and something the White House or Homeland considers vital and thoroughly infiltrates, until the place contains so many top-heavy constructs, as well as snarls, and there are so many of these places around the world, for example high finance and the insurance industry.

In fact, the place has no other workers, just piles and piles of tightly packed tall tippable rubble, such as pull on a small item, which looks quite secure then a huge dangerous wall falls inward.

And this humid place, it is as if someone opens an oven door with barely enough room to squeeze inside.

Of which from behind, he urges her forward to tour the facility, and she resists each time, primarily because of the enormous dingy clutter, and mountains of it, as well as that earlier name incident in front of the building, all those weapons, standing in

the Deep South, Confederate flags, and various bumper stickers, such as *I'M NOT RACIST, I'M JUST EDUCATED.*
*THE SOUTH WILL RISE AGAIN.*
*IMMIGRANTS – GET OUT.*
*SHOOT FIRST, ASK QUESTIONS LATER.*
*MOMMA'S PACKING HEAT.*
*YES, TRUCKERS DO OWN THE ROAD.*

And yet, she eventually does, however her face shows considerable stress in a series of stages, which the man does not notice as he talks and talks with great pride about the facility, and he talks as if a soliloquy, a broadcast, a life history speech with few natural pauses.

And of equal importance each pile has no rhythm or reason, no known organizational system or rational.

In fact, it contains mostly overgrowth yet without an index, and in a way it resembles nature, roots, a rhizome system, yet lacks a story, a throughline, as well as paired opposites, dynamics, companions and the dependents: life!

And once well into the system, which contains so many elaborate twists, turns and switchbacks, she reaches a point of no return, a return-by-reference, or return to forever.

So much so, panic arrives and the heart pounds and pounds.

In fact, it causes a taste to linger on the palette, a taste of plasma, as well as a mineral ion feel and something else—something, maybe a taste of the common metal, iron, a transitional metal, which oddly enough has a certain harmony, the harmonics of d-block and the d-orbital subshell.

And yet something else happens, something.

Calm arrives, and very much so.

Then a completely unexpected spark arrives, a profound realized truth about these enormous plies of junk, this trap.

She stands among a deep mathematical beauty, and ever so spectacular version, a tree of life, and not that classic version, not a religious structure or system, something else, some other great mystery.

# CHAPTER 30

Eventually she recovers inside that deep mathematical beauty and notices a complete diving suit here and there among tall rubble.

All of which seem quite remarkable, and a manufacturer fully dedicated to the subject.

And of equal note, off to the side stands an ADS replica, built by Carmagnolle brothers in 1882, said "the first anthropomorphic design."

"Would you like a full explanation?"

As a result, her face lights, "Hell yes!"

And once done, she exits the storage area yet each foot placement tries to gingerly avoid trouble, avoid a Jenga or dominos action, such as one wrong touch and much of the production facility as well as storage might collapse.

Then once outside she says "I know very little about diving.

"This suit would be a gift, for a friend.

"She recently graduated from marine biology school."

"Graduated in Massachusetts and a treasure hunter I bet?

"I call always tell a treasure hunter, always.

"They hear a story, spark from a rumor, read a book, find a map, imagine then obsess."

"No, no," she says while patting the air.

"Nothing like that—coral reefs, marine biology, and stuff like that."

"Yeah, sure, coral reefs," wink-wink then he points at his finest custom diving suit, WASP, glass-reinforced plastic, and he lists features, such as height, width, support frame, weight, power source, as well as deployment systems, propulsion, video systems, then life support, safety systems, hull, communications, limbs, manipulators, and price.

Of which, the cost staggers, "Really.

"That's expensive?

"Is there a less expensive system, a more mobile version, one a person can walk about more freely?"

Then she shows crude drawings, deliberately crude to hide her real mission and secret, yet would show more than enough detail that might spark a new lead, or at least more ideas on how to rethink her mission.

He nods, "Yes, I can."

And she leans slightly forward.

"What you're referring to is made from cast and machined aluminum, no umbilical cord, and it would still have elaborate pressure joints, to allow considerable articulation while maintaining an internal pressure of one atmosphere, and be able to operate at very deep dives, up to 2,300 feet for eighty hours, as well as use no special gas mixtures and scrub carbon.

"I can make it" then he quotes a price.

Her eyes widen and she says, "I see," and feels a compelling need to exit. "Well, clearly beyond my budget and needs, her needs.

"Coral reef studies, that's it."

Then he edges toward her and into personal space, which disconcerts her.

"You're the sixth person this week looking for those features, and they seemed in a hurry.

"All of them had thick accents, such as from Germany, Norway, Denmark, France, Australia, and Japan."

So Agrippa scrambles to think of something and eventually says, "It must have been that recent *Popular Science* article sparking interest," and she half chuckles.

"I fully appreciate your time and effort.

"Thank you, Roscoe—I mean Jimmy."

And for a moment he sizzles then recovers, "It's Jimmy.

"And if you leave your number, I can put you on our mailing list."

Of which she does, yet gives a fake name and address then exits.

Moments later, a fellow worker arrives from deep within the rubble, the mathematical beauty and says to Jimmy, "Treasure hunter.

"She's onto something, something big."

"Yes, I agree."

"Call that guy, the visiting subcontractor, Chris, he's in the back. Chris, Chris Overbeck, and let him know."

Eventually all three huddle.

# CHAPTER 31

Not much later, Agrippa quickly backs out of the parking lot, drives down that dirt road and hits one bone-jarring-pothole after another, and each time scraps the rental car bottom.

Eventually, something falls off, and again, a part, maybe a considerable one or two.

However, she seems distracted from events and has no interest in stopping, climbing under the car on a dirt road and determining if they represent vital parts then collecting them.

Regardless, and once near the airport, the plane delays then cancels, the last flight of the day, and to make matters worse, a Natchez Convention Center event adds difficulty finding a room.

So, after traveling about the city, then outskirts, she locates a no-frills motel room for thirty-two dollars a night, the type of place with no flat screen TV, pool or other fancy amenities. Yet it has an icemaker and more importantly, a bar nearby, less than a block away.

"Perfect.

"I need a drink.

"In fact, I need a few potent drinks, such as one quick potent drink after another, of distilled pneuma, psyche and wit, yes, self-medication, such as a popular grog, a powerful one with a vital spark; yes, a potent drink, which might rejuvenate the mind, body and soul, and one that serves as a proven tonic, one said effective, efficient, precise and balanced, yet more importantly, it must produce a classic buzz, and not the cultural elite version, not a post-meal lull brandy or *aqua vitae*, or gentian spirit, bitter or *digestif*.

"I want a proven buzz that matches the universal wave function, the universe, paradise, and the way it should have been in the very beginning."

Not much later, after the hotel registration, she walks to the bar and pass several neat motorcycle rows, then into a tightly packed bar, quite, and squeezes between so many people which takes a considerable time and effort, until she finally arrives at the counter and says, "A Long Island Iced Tea."

Regardless, a warm beer arrives.

"A Long Island Iced Tea."

Another warm beer arrives.

"Ah, a Long Island Iced Tea."

A third warm beer arrives, and all appear flat, no foam whatsoever then bartender says, "That's sixty dollars."

Of which, it takes her aback.

"I didn't order a beer.

"Sixty dollars?" and her demeanor shifts from puzzled to assertive, while leaning forward, as eyes narrow and the manner seems slightly annoyed.

The bartender does the same and says, "Pay the sixty dollars, then my friends and I will drink your beers in front of you, then you get up and leave, got it?"

And that shocks her awake, as most people go through a typical day on autopilot, coasting, hoping to arrive in the promised land, finally.

Such as a person drives home and does not remember any significant details about that trip.

Or, a person walks from one end of the house to another, then once there, cannot remember the trip or purpose yet bumps nothing, such as on the tree of habit, tree of life, tree-depth, tree-graded space or on the mental table of judgment?

Or a more important fact, no one can arrive twice at the exact same point in universal space, which might represent some of the disorientation, frustration and conflict, from going to a new place every second inside the universe, or new segment on a single complex string or algebraic bubble, or are they one and the same?

However, the sheer number and weight of present as well as past clues jolt her, especially standing in the Deep South, in historical Natchez, Mississippi, with Confederate flags, gun racks in pickup trucks, bumper stickers that include, *I'M NOT RACIST, I'M JUST EDUCATED.*

*THE SOUTH WILL RISE AGAIN.*

*IMMIGRANTS – GET OUT.*

*SHOOT FIRST, ASK QUESTIONS LATER.*

*MOMMA'S PACKING HEAT.*

*YES, TRUCKERS DO OWN THE ROAD.*

Then she really looks at the bartender for the first time, and there stands a tall bear of a man named Little Tate, who also wears a t-shirt that says, *IF YOU SMILE, I'LL PUNCH YOU IN THE FACE*, and chews something, then neatly spits to the side.

Of which, Agrippa looks around the bar and finally notices a tense mood, as well as bad omens, run-down decor, beer-stained pool tables, grisly people, rough weathered faces, a collection of mostly hardcore bikers and rednecks, a rare place these differing groups agree to gather, drink cheap booze and fight it out, and do so fair and square.

Just as importantly at the door way, a sign clearly says, *FIVE DOLLAR COVER CHARGE*, and the sheer gravity arrives, then distant look on her face, "Oh.

"I see.

"Oh my!"

Then much of the crowd edges closer, and a few hardcore rednecks step within range and one of them say, "Massachusetts?

"Really?

"Do you have any idea where you are?

"The Deep South.

"And you stroll in here like you own the place, la dee da, and ignore the cover charge, push your way through the crowd of locals, step front and center then call for a sissy drink, a Long Island Iced Tea.

"Did you read the entrance sign?"

She concerns, yet avoids revealing much, as apparently the sign was partially blocked by a mass of humanity, a bit under seven foot and weighting approximately one buttermilk biscuit short of 370 pounds.

Then he moves and the full sign clearly displays entrance requirements: *FIVE DOLLAR COVER CHARGE.*

Again Agrippa thinks yet reveal little, *Oh my!*

*Trouble.*

Elsewhere and outside her motel room, Chris Overbeck and another man arrives, don gloves, and carefully look about.

Then with specialized tools, they easily manipulate the motel door lock open, and Chris wildly searches the room for each and every possible hiding place, which leaves a considerable ruin, while the other man stands guard.

Upon exiting he says, "Nothing."

So eventually, Chris picks the car door lock and immediately grabs the rental agreement, then looks through every aspect of the car interior, and with a lever pull opens the trunk and wildly digs inside one bag after another.

There he finds a few diving suit components, which include a panel, clasps, bolts, protective plates and a puzzling spent cartridge, something similar to an eighty-eight gram threaded paintball CO-two cartridge.

"Yes.

"Jackpot, Solms."

And the other man says in a Norwegian accent, "I found more than enough.

"However, what the hell is this?" And he examines the cartridge, hesitates, then sniffs, recoils, as well as carefully looks, squints, rubs at vague markings, then takes a small whiff and says, "Yes, nice touch.

"I love it.

"Clever."

Then Solms pokes at him.

"What?"

"We have a sedative, well, more than that.

"It was incorporated into the breathing system."

"What?"

"Yes, it's a complex sedative, yet for atonement, the harmonics of a well field mental system, and all those benefits and natural harmony of a very smooth transition, a true lost art, and one without all those seams, and all done as if a noble experiment that honors the classics, and yet as a bold new frontier of a threshold adventure."

What?"

"It bends the mind.

"To improve abstract thought, especially the executive function, and a process that alters neurochemicals, such as neurotransmitters, enzymes and hormones."

"What?"

"A smart drugs, quite, and designed to manage the brain's supply of neurochemicals such as neurotransmitters, enzymes, and hormones.

"And it improves circulation, carbon removal, decreases claustrophobia, while enabling a person to remain alert, in fact, better than alert.

"However, there is a downside, so hold the celebration, because nearly all of the breathing components are missing as well as the key companion gases, nootropic agent, formula mixture and hoses."

So these two men grab as much as possible, especially DNA evidence, which in a way represents a history of the last human species, and nature, the universe, to grab?

Regardless, they mean well, in their own way, as nature has a certain reach though claim?

# CHAPTER

M eanwhile in that bar, an old-school biker named Bertha in black leather, a classic tough, uncompromising person of pure intimidation, rudely pushes her way through the crowd, especially with elbows, which others grumble then realize it's her then pat the air as coolant, just in case she turns toward them.

And she says, "I got this."

Of which no one disagrees, not a few longtime rivals, who now have an opportunity and forum to showcase a true comeback story against her, a chance for glory, a public trial by fire, a fistic revival, and do so in fist city with plenty of witnesses, and not a he-said or she-said of a back alley fight, such as late at night or when the bar begins to close at that circadian rhythm primetime slot, 2:00 a.m. with half-drunk witnesses, which creates doubt, such as sanction a founding myth, a collective hope and dream.

And the crowd completely agrees with her, which seems quite rare indeed for hardcore bikers and rednecks, and so quickly as they form a circle with an eight-foot radius, as eight seems right for a transition, for penance then resurrection.

"Go get her Bertha."

And she warms up, cracks knuckle, neck and back then circles clockwise, and cheers-call Southern style, the way it is supposed to be, the world according to the South, such as with hoots, and hollers.

Someone yells, "The North versus the Deep South!" And the crowd agrees, reaches an agreement.

Then Agrippa says, "Oh.

"Oh my!

"Wait a minute," and arms pat the air.

"Hold on.

"There must be a misunderstanding.

"I just want a potent drink, a vital spark, a classic buzz.

"Hell, right now I'd settle for a sixty dollar warm beer, yes: a flat beer, no foam."

However, the mob would have none of that.

And as the former naval commander nearly completes those words, Bertha lands a powerful one-two-punch, left-right, which the first buckles Agrippa's knees and the second causes her to reel back and go to one knee.

So much so, stars arrive, not celebrities, not real celebrities, people with true star power, such as a diva or divo, or the political equivalent, not the professional panderer, or someone on the A, B, C or D-list, which might have the most oh-so-juicy scandals, and anything to feel alive during this slog in the massive underclass, the underutilized, as an expendable, and not those stars that illuminate a night sky or ones that sit at the very edge of the universe, the edge of the algebraic bubble, but strange ones that dart inside her darkened field of vision, ones with a distinct pattern, an elongated L-shaped movement here and there.

Of equal significance the mob electrifies and cheers, as some feed on it, gain degrees of satisfaction as well as pleasure from pain and destruction?

Have you ever studied a fight crowd in great detail, really studied in a comprehensive way?

Here and now, some people turn to one another with lit faces, fully illuminate, and say "Love it, really, love it."

And a few shift between horror and true pathos.

Others smile with a wide beam.

Some stand numb and yet some stand inattentive, seem elsewhere, and more than a few clearly imagine being in that fight then quick-twitch in anticipation, taunt, throw mock punches, bob and weave, then immediately claim an unparalleled glory, as if they found a cure for cancer or saved a yellow school bus filled with children from disaster or built one of the eight wonders of the world.

Regardless, Agrippa slowly blinks and carefully studies the stars.

In fact, she looks for pattern and purpose, and where is this place, where are these stars, what part of the mind?

Then a small portion of her senses return yet she had no idea of who, what, where, when, or why.

Oddly enough she chuckles a bit and follows the stars, even points at a few and now smells licorice, lemon balm, peppermint, allspice, cinnamon and cloves.

Then vivid memories of her father arrive, and telling the story of how she got that name, Marcus Vipsanius Agrippa, well, because he wanted a baby boy, and in the worst possible way.

And each time he told that story, his face would light with immense joy, which she amazed at his reaction then carefully studied his face.

Especially as he remembers the doctors and nurses who leaned ever so close to the newborn, and they ogled, as well as made all those goo-goo baby talk noises, then the little girl born with two clinched fists seriously considered these people and in great detail then eventually released a single finger. Yes, the finger! That finger! And at that moment her father realized absolute satisfaction then hatched a plan, to lay low, very, and whatever the mother named her, he would somehow, someway rename her after Marcus Vipsanius Agrippa, his hero.

Then more memories jolt loose from that powerful one-two-punch, a left-right, the Bertha express.

And she remembers all those warnings by family, friends, and especially during her Navy boot camp training. Where they warn about her index of character, about things taken for granted, about her tone deftness on a whole range of issues, which included the impulse to barge into a situation without a careful measure of the subtle and dynamic, as well as the need for deftness.

They warn about this day, when all these habits and events would converge then produce a fall, a fall from grace.

However, if a person wants to change, to improve, they must carefully remove habits and personality traits, as well as do so systematically, especially the bad ones, as they might represent the best of the best, the best part of a person as odd as that might sound. For example, the bad traits might serve as critical infrastructure and other functions, some of which do so in an unknown and unobservable way yet have a profound purpose as well as interdependency with other vital traits. Such as, they act as a deterrent, to avoid showing weakness among others.

And the personality represents a complex construct, especially the social constructs, because of all those scripts, and so many roles, so many scripts a person speak as well as live, and often many scripts at the same time, as a person must serve so many powerful masters at the same time, so many constructs or else, which often seem quite impossible, as well as draconian, obsessive, and fickle, and in a place filled with various major as well as minor overlords, with authoritarians. Such say one wrong word or move and you start at the bottom, that long climb out of poverty again.

And people often mentally crack from stress, and go to la-la land, go wherever a person travels when the mind snaps, really snaps from enormous pressure and loses the focal point, bearing, mission, as well as all those roles and scripts assigned to them since birth—for example, when the focal point jolts from a fist, and fails to marshal internal regions of the mind, body and soul, and mental regions often at war with one other, or when the focal point falls into an unfamiliar region of the mind. When it lands somewhere in the vast subconscious stockpile, among the biological superstructure, among the machinery, mechanics, and strategic reserves, and among the places most people take for granted, and it could quite possibly land in between personal baggage.

And often people mentally crack then show one emotion after another, which includes a wild-eyed craze, a real out-of-mind look, followed by complete calm then concern, worry, alarm, panic, evasive, petrified, and calm, acceptance, satisfied, happy, giddy, elated, then clinically insane as a profound realization appears of the face.

It happens, as many societies deliberately make life hell on earth with impossible situations, with hype, escalation, and all those elaborate contracts, as well as scripts, and jump through one hoop after another, such as here and there, then make one agreement after another, and often with a subtle or obvious gestures, with a blink, or nod, or until the hand cramps, becomes a claw, not quite *I, Claudius*, but I promise to serve, often they want forever—yes, forever. Then you might get the essentials, such as fresh air, springwater, real food, and love, that gift, that substantial treasure, maybe, as compared with artificial whatnot. But at what cost, for the essentials, as a person moves about with that very complex tethering system, which often pulls a person far away from their original intent as well as natural aspiration, and with even more restricted degrees of freedom.

And it often takes so many adjustments to get there, to get the essentials. Of equal importance, the adjustments seem endless, all those adjustments, and by the time a person finally arrives, he or she cannot focus on the here and now, just on all those complex twists and turns, on all that commotion, as well as propaganda or commercialism, and those elaborate terms to get there, all those elaborate verbal and written contracts, as well as tethers, and this also applies to other aspirations as well.

So, a person might lose that rare golden moment, when it finally arrives, such as love and paradise, or "Love and Happiness?"

# CHAPTER 33

Regardless, as well as here and now while still seeing stars, Agrippa growls at the Navy boot camp memories.

In fact, she digs in her metaphorical heels and grumble about this and that, about the blue Navy Smurf outfits, and having to donate her prized clothing to charity, about the first uniform, as well as needing "special instructions" and "individual training" for being "a willful person."

Then she growls at the male petty officer memory, who orders her to take off the gas mask and sing both verses of "Anchors Aweigh," as a clown, a spoof yet show of shows.

Well, she growls because women must make more than a few additional adjustments, compromises, such as lose a few traits, a few components of true greatness, those pesky things, such as a sense of compassion and mercy for the weak, victim and prey.

Then not satisfied with her Navy performance, which lacks flair and gusto, he orders her to do the entire process two more times under the banner of "special instructions."

"Grrr."

Of which here and now, the bar crowd notices the odd behavior then react in various ways.

Then Agrippa recovers from those two crisp punches, tries to focus, blinks, eventually looks about and sees a mob that shouts, cheers, and prods Bertha.

Even her frenemies show complete support, those longtime rivals, who could now take this opportunity and forum to showcase their true comeback story against her, a chance for glory, a public trial by fire, a fistic revival with plenty of witnesses, and not a he-said or she-said of a back alley fight, such as late at night or when the bar begins to close at that circadian rhythm primetime slot, 2:00 a.m. with half-drunk witnesses, which creates doubt, such as sanction a founding myth, a collective hope and dream, or memory, dream, genre, situation, as well as high concept adventure then region of stability, to a heal, such as next to an exceptional artesian spring, in a secular or sacred form of Gan Eden, Avalon, Baltia, Shambhala, Beyul or El Dorado, or some other official transcendent paradise with really good water, such as what was loosely described in *The Travels of Sir John Mandeville* or by Juan Ponce de León, the snapback effect of vitality-restoring waters, and that cool sip, which redeems and restores original intent, aspiration, and reserve of spark then sip again, under a tree of life, of knowledge, or a localized version, a one-of-a-kind, an idiosyncratic, and that opportunity as well as forum to showcase a true comeback story.

Regardless, as well as here and now, what could possibly explain that process, of how rivals switch loyalty to Bertha?

How is that possible, and so quickly?

Just as significantly, some in the crowd grin, show bug eyes, beads of sweat, and tell Agrippa to beg for her life.

And others stand ready to rush in with their best curbside stomp, a fully animated curbside stomp, the type where an arm whips about in the air for balance.

So much so, it appears the day of reckoning, whether fate, bad luck, randomness of nature, poor judgment, cumulative transgression, karma or a reliance on impulse.

As a result, isolated, alone and disenfranchised, a realization bolt strikes her chest, stomach pit, and skin, an ever so profound realization of *déjà vu*, done, as in *finito*.

And with this full realization, her soul shivers, and eyes widen as if on the very edge of a great cliff, some final precipice of existence, such as a dangerous crag with chasm, which offers a precarious edge of crumble then steep drop, into no more excuses, into the impossible mystery of frontier justice.

Then she notices the sublime aspects of horror.

So much so, hair stands and individualizes on the arms, neck, and scalp. As if each hair casts a unique vote, and is that possible, can each hair follicle communicate, can they vote?

All of which translates into an impulse, she should stand and run as fast as possible, somewhere, anywhere and now, yes, right now, go-go-go, then run for dear life, and not run like a girl—you know, where the arms do that funny thing and move in that unusual way, and what is that movement?

What is the scientific or evolutionary reason for the running style?

However, something else happens, something.

# CHAPTER 34

❖ ◈ ❖

A nd with all these grim notices, the mob ready to surge, to demand payback, pain and destruction, she could totally unravel, could become hysterical, could weep uncontrollably and blubber, then say "Woe is me, the world is out to get me!"

Instead she says with an ever so cool and calm demeanor, "Yes, this must be the place, I see," as eyes widen.

"The great threshold adventure, the great frontier, and a place that tests, as well as puts the identity in full crisis at this enthalpy threshold, yes, an identity foreclosure, a critical phase transition during the identity versus role crisis of the self, with those mysteries of various internal and external separations, all those nuances.

"Yes, this is a place where anything is possible—anything, even true glory and greatness."

And with this realization, she frees, frees from pride, from petty emotion and especially from this event as a personal act, that technique.

However, something else happens, something.

The first of four iron bands restricting her heart releases, a mental construct, restriction, an ever so stale script, also known as baggage; and some might say inside her trouble tree.

Of equal significance, and oddly enough the air suddenly seems fresher, even in this beer-stained room, a place where people often bump with an elbow, such as beer. And things spill yet rarely does the staff meticulously clean this place, just the opposite, as a complete cleaning would remove the atmosphere, *ambience, mise-en-scene*, well, not said with those words, as the staff often points to this fact at rare meetings, and "Why meticulously clean?"

Regardless for Agrippa, things become quite vivid, and for the next few minutes, she becomes a vehicle for the sublime, and reaches full accord with nature, as the mob to her becomes a single entity, a song, a universal harmonic string, a tether to the collective unconscious.

In addition, she nods yes to it, to life, and to each and every one who would look directly into her eyes at that new keenly realized state.

And oddly enough, many people in the bar react with a unique puzzle, as that state of mind rarely exists, well because the system does not train people to think like that. It trains them to join a quagmire, an escalation, life in a quandary, a catch-22, Cornelian dilemma, no-win situation, Pyrrhic victory-based system, and slowly decline in search of a livable wage, or work as an intern, and understudy or as *The Dresser*, a reluctant benchwarmer in someone else's storyline, the narrative, especially at the local level, or live under a storyline, sometimes dozens of them at the same time, created by social mandates or by the tremendously powerful, as well as dangerous people, places and things. Where, they set the agenda as well as the storylines. So, a passenger tries to safely navigate among them, or under them, such as one wrong word or script variation and the powers-that-be might drop something on you, for instance a red brick building on fire. And a system, proxy or mob might polarize and form because of the smallest thing, for trivia or factoid, and very much so, as in trivial pursuit with exceptionally dangerous consequences for minutia, for a small inflective error, from a blink at the wrong time, from a failure to cheer loud enough with the system, the power-that-be, and on cue, on the mark, and for a very small freedom of expression.

Of equal importance, Agrippa has one perceptual shift after another, and notices more things, such as how people play and stoke the mob, their tone, voice, pattern, manner and the verbal clue.

So Agrippa stands and says, "Yes," and eyes narrow as she finds the mob's center of gravity, where it gains sustenance and vigor, then studies the crucial elements that hold it together, those people, such as the lord of the flies, then motions them forward, one by one.

In fact, she warmly invites them forward.

Of which, it startle them, the unusual calm of an invitation among the storm, the singling out while in profane and sacred social space, during this crisis of the ceremony, this manner of crossing the threshold, taking on aspects of a sacred marriage yet decupled that way.

And she motions forward, not you or you, and yes you with a subtle head nods and hand motion as if a welcoming into the sublime.

Soon they arrive, front and center as honored guests, to a place with the best possible ceremonial significates, into the innermost circle, to a place quite mob noticeable, especially their every movement, every twitch.

Then she quickly confirms everyone's readiness, which seems to surprise a considerable number of people, yet no one disagrees, even as Bertha, the old-school biker babe in that classic black leather outfit, nods *whatever*, and the crowd shout, "Go get her Bertha," who circles counterclockwise and practices a few killer combinations, ones designed for an instant knockout, where the person would drop straight to the floor, collapses into a heap.

Yet Agrippa offers a handshake, a fresh start and fully extends her hand, as well as leans far forward with a special courtesy of full honor, which Bertha huffs, refuses, then spits off to the side, and Agrippa notices with no emotion, pride, or pettiness, as that would represent a personal act.

And they collide in a hockey-style clench then struggle to gain an advantage.

So much so each struggle tries to gain a special grip, an advantage, such as S, T, three-finger and Gable.

Then with the slightest opening, Bertha delivers a tremendous shot to the stomach, rib then head, which causes considerable damage, so Agrippa moves closer, into a tight clench then somehow eventually delivers a jaw-jolting elbow uppercut, and again and again.

Of which, these soon leave Bertha in an untenable position, not stunned but completely unable to defend tremendous shots, which have an unknown effect.

That happens in life.

So, she separates into a good old-fashioned fistfight, old-school style, a rockem sockem, a toe-to-toe slugfest glory.

And within thirty seconds, it morphs into a combination of Muay Thai, and a Greco-Roman fight.

Then Agrippa spits out a blood tooth.

Moments later, within close quarter in-fighting, each of them land fast crisp shots over and over.

So much so neither of them could maintain that damage or pace.

As a result, Agrippa establishes a full clinch then fakes a motion to release and quickly escape backwards.

And instead leaps forward with a brutal short right hook to the jaw, which causes Bertha to collapse straight down in an instant collapse, and completely out.

Immediately, her friends as well as frenemies rush and apply recovery assistance, certain procedures, and not recovery from a bias, not recovery from a cult.

Then the formal Naval commander motions to a guy in that select group, one who sports "a full Brett Kiesel beard" and t-shirt back that says, *I'M NOT RACIST, I'M JUST EDUCATED*, the one with the most mob sway, most able to keep the mob in a whipped state, the guy with wild eyes, dominant, one who offers over-the-top gestures and makes sudden moves.

"By the way, this represents no disrespect to Brett Kiesel.

So, she welcomes him into the ceremonial pit.

Of which, he sees, sparks, considers, looks to others, brags, squints, measures, nods, relays to the group an over-the-top eagerness and approaches, and all the while plays to the mob with bold gestures, to whip them up, and meticulously looks for clues to stoke the flames higher and still higher, and the crowd erupts from each deliberate well-timed cue.

Some people master that skill of how to excite the mob, how to escalate.

And of equal importance, he seems as if a monster of a man, bulging insane eyes, the older brother of the bartender, the first of seven brothers who normally carry around a legendary two by four to settle disputes.

All of which cause members of the crowd to grow giddy and they turn to one another, spark and inflate.

It seems as if he gave all of them a raise in pay, a living wage, or save a yellow school bus filled with preschoolers, or won the Nobel Prize, that type of joy.

And the mob chants his name, "Big Tate! Big Tate!"

Then people bet, as many people say "Why not earn a considerable fortune on conflict, such as dynamite?"

So, they exchange odds.

Arguments polarize.

The giddy tremble.

The greedy look for a monopoly.

The impulsive twitch from phantoms.

And the cruel gain enormous pleasure at the thought of inflicting pain.

Then moments later, this man fakes a bull rush and smirks, which the crowd loves and roars with delight, especially with each over-the-top act, as he whips them up with well-timed showmanship gestures, and they turn to one another in full admiration, as well as respect of the way it should be.

And he motions one way then lands a solid punch the other way, straight up the middle then moments later with another trick, he delivers another solid one-two, a left-right, which she catches some of the force from her guard, yet each punch arrives with accurate and numbing authority.

Then he systematically drives her about at will, which plays well to the crowd, who cheer with considerable admiration, especially as he often cues them with over-the-top gestures, to fully animate.

Eventually a punch causes her knees to buckle, so he swarms and lands a series of power shots that include hooks and brutal uppercuts, which cause her to grab a wrist, arm, elbow, and neck, anything to gain her bearings.

And special grips allow her to rest inside, then with over-hooks when necessary, even during one struggle after another, as the secret is a breathing technique, to avoid an adrenaline dump, ask any Greco-Roman wrestler, or refer to *prāṇāyāma* techniques.

Just as importantly, one tremendous struggle after another appears to slow Big Tate considerably, and the back of the t-shirt, *I'M NOT RACIST, I'M JUST EDUCATED* contains a considerable amount of sweat, as if he worked in a sweatshop for years, at below a livable wage, to "earn sweat equity," that phrase often given to a generation, and that type of debilitating look after years of work yet a system fails to deliver then devalues the money or blames it on someone else, blames it on the usual suspects.

Regardless, the mob chants his name, "Big Tate! Big Tate!" and tremendous pride amps, which he transmits to the crowd with over-the-top gestures, as well as ever so wild eyes and they love it, truly loved it then he shouts, "Look Ma, I'm on top of the world!"

As a result he breaks that fancy grip, yet she delivers three short elbows to his jaw, so he gains considerable distance then spits a bloody tooth, of which the crowd truly celebrates, especially as he full-beam smiles, and in a way that show the bloody gap then nods yes to this truly great adventure.

And all of a sudden, it becomes an all-out, toe-to-toe slugfest, a true glory.

However, he eventually gets the best of each exchange, which force her to retreat, and sidestep away from his power, and again, as she seems unable to keep him at bay and the crowd cheers.

So she switches to southpaw, and this affords more recovery time, because some people seem unable to switch mindsets for whatever reason, unable switch perspectives, to other social constructs.

As a result, he seems awkward, unable to read her perspective, overreaches, and the timing seems off, as well as prone to feints.

Eventually, she maneuvers to a position front and center of those honored guests, where the innermost circle can clearly see those twitch-sensitive image makers, tastemakers or troublemakers if you will, which depends on perspective, yes, as some might say rascals, misunderstood, lovable rogues, and other might say the righteous. Again it depends on perspective, on how you frame the constitution, and especially who writes history, such as men as founding fathers with no mention of founding mothers, or grandparents, or a system founded by women, or some other trait, as human history has so many examples.

And of greater importance, these honored guests have the best field of vision and best possible ceremonial significance in relationship to the crowd, and who can see every twitch.

Then moments later, she rushes inside and fakes a clinch, then delivers a solid spinning back elbow to the jaw, and another and another, which causes Big Tate to collapse straight down, into a heap and out cold.

Of which the crowd quickly loses energy as an unusual calm arrives.

However, a few people shout praise about these poetic strikes, as if they were a series of exceptional poetic phrases within the dramatic structure, an uncommon narrative arc of exploration with three acts, as she stumbles through the crowd, arrives at the bar, digs deep into her pockets, pays the Northern fine, takes a few slips of flat beer and quietly says, "All that cheering, I thought someone discovered a cure for cancer or saved a busload of children from going off a cliff, and why is that?

"Have you noticed, doctors no longer cure anything.

"When is the last time they cured something?

"Scurvy?

"Polio?

"And yet they spend record amounts of money on tests and research" then she exits the bar, stumbles the long walk back, and it eventually becomes clear, the car had been vandalized; yet she does not overreact, just quietly closes the trunk as well as door then enters the room, and falls fast asleep fully clothed.

# CHAPTER 35

Elsewhere, Bonnie remembers the last meal, that box, which contained two large pulled pork sandwiches, coleslaw and potato salad, all homemade, and underneath sat braised beef short ribs, twice-baked russet potatoes with sour cream, cheddar cheese, extra crispy bacon, sated onions and butter, as well as grilled corn-on-the-cob, of which the sight and smell nearly caused her to drift into a delightful place, a savory world.

So in search of morsels, she digs through that box one more time, and finds a considerable amount of extra crispy bacon bits, heavenly bits, which seem best eaten slowly, nibbled on, one bit at a time, to savor with eyes closed.

"I love it, extra crispy bacon, especially the taste and crunch.

"Yes, quite satisfying, as it seems to improve nearly all things, such as an ever so dull garden salad, steamed vegetables, sandwiches, and casseroles to name a few things."

Then moments later, a fully determined look arrives, of no-nonsense then she travels towards nearest the mansion property marker, to get that first geodetic survey metal plate inscribed with property details.

And this new effort takes her through one ultradense forest section after another, each with heavily thorn thickets, with wait-a-minute-shrubs that grab, inflict pain, and cause flinch to protect the face and eyes.

So much so, these hook-shaped thorns poke skin, and snag, as well as precariously catch clothing, and eventually cause limbs to swell, especially faces, hands, arms, and legs from those toxic thorns.

In fact, they balloon, and soon develop a grotesque appearance—such that legs and arms appear as thick ghastly things, and something not quite human.

So much so, mobility declines as limbs cramp and allow an odd run-hobble.

Ultimately, these limbs appear freakish, the type a person should not look at and especially not dwell on, as it might trigger the mind to lose orientation and panic then surrender into a dangerous state of shock, or at a minimum, the mind might unravel and think very wild thoughts about these grotesque limbs.

It might unlock memories and personal baggage, unlock all those known flaws and imperfections, then flood the mind with vivid images and other wholly irrational things, such as the life of an outcast, an outsider, life as a true freak, who has become the other, become a thing, or an it—at such a point where choices narrow and narrow until a person becomes isolated. Or worse yet, the system herds them into a sideshow with the other freaks, forces them to join a classic sideshow, a new age P. T. Barnum event or live in a cabinet of curiosities, a *Wunderkammer*, or in a modern-day version of the Black Scorpion or Jim Rose Circus, a lollapalooza festival, or forces them into an old-time revival show, with a barker on some local circuit that visits rural towns. And people can pay a single price of admission, and even take their children for a cautionary lesson of enter the big top tent then gawk at human oddities, at the freaks, at the working acts, so obey the system or else, because this might happen to you.

Regardless, she frantically odd-hobbles in search of the property marker while mumbling this and that, mostly things unfit for print.

Yet the dog travels elsewhere.

And after five hours, she appears absolutely lost then accidentally arrives at that unusual tree with hybrid aspects, which includes traits associated with oak, peach, beech, hazel, ash, eucalyptus, willow, sycamore, almond, baobab and sandalwood, as well as acacia with thorny pods, shevaga, assattha, fig, kalpavriksha, thuja and yew, together with something unlike what a person might expect near the Well of Souls.

The tree shows phase transitions—those seams, stages, miscibility gaps and degrees associated with liminal, with the structure of identity, time and common space, such as the axiomatic system, special sets and Cartesian products of both spatial and temporal dimensions, which concern the moment, period and epoch, and a new way of individuation, as well as aspects that seem constantly stuck or pinned to the here and now.

In addition, this tree has something else not easily quantifiable, for instance sections with matter that seems out of phase, as well as aspects that seem ambiguous and produce a considerable temporal thrownness, or luminiferous ether as well as disorientation as if a mid-ritual event, and just after a person or thing exits the original state of identity, time, and community; that threshold structure and process of a new way, yet not easily quantifiable, and possibly an aspect of subspace, as in some integral part and nuisance location within spacetime, one distinct and yet coexistent with normal space. As subspace domains and normal space all represent available locations within the universe, or as if within a metaverse system, the protocol stack of the universe bulkhead or series of bulkheads, or a multiverse, or blank verse stack.

And some tree branches contain what appear as night-flowering jasmine, grape clusters, as well as bonsai attachments, phylogenetic catalysts, and other plants attach in some form of symbiosis, a set of persistent biological interactions, which maybe mutualistic, commensalistic, parasitic or something else, and yet they all resemble a stockpile of scripts, a microcosm or community, such as a community organization, agent, garden or theater, a power set that includes an empty set or seat.

In addition, this tree sits squarely with the four cardinal directions, as if a boxing-the-compass-device, and it also has a heavily fortified vacant station, station port, reference stream, reference point indentation, permanent dwell, and a place for demarcation transactions, for start and end a transaction that uses begin, commit, and rollback methods if need be, such as roll back time and space, and yet with an aspect to stand guard and not go beyond, as well as a place of structural and territorial integrity with a separation of powers, and on one side as a well-field schema, altered state, another way or artistic backstory, which translates on entrance into this field, as if a complex bilateral language function and tonal adjustment, a prosodic translation, a simultaneous function, and just outside that field, a tremendous form of facticity or thrownness.

So avoid this place, or risk everything, as it might remove a person from the timeline, from history, such as rush into that tree influence, through those stages of, and something an articulate scientist, musician or poet might better describe, and with far more precision regarding all those obvious and subtle aspects, for example, as if a tetration analytic extension, and all those individual complex states, some temporal, and others seems to transcend all conventional language and thought.

It resembles a universal entanglement, mostly unseen, as well as the real science and "mythology of lost," because there appears no decent direct route through this complex estate.

Of considerable note, in a nearby grotto sits a brand-new and fully crated Hammond B-3 organ, clearly marked *PRIVATE PROPERTY* in fire-engine red stencil, as well as *PLAY IT AND YOU WILL DIE.*

In addition, bit of leaves, twigs, and the debris cover it, which give the appearance it has been there for ten, twenty, even thirty years or more, and likely the golden age when Hammond B-3 ruled the world.

And regardless of her condition, she feels feisty, yes, in fact defiant, and could play if need be, such as Jimmy Mcgriff's, "I Got a Woman", to evoke a true revival, a restoration.

Yes, stand up, right now, and celebrate, that type of defiance.

# CHAPTER 36

Before Bonnie realizes, she seems caught in a tremendous force that surrounds the tree, a certain structural and territorial integrity with a separation of powers, and one side has a well-field schema, altered state, another way or artistic backstory, maybe a mixed selection of, which translates on entrance into this field, as if a complex bilateral language function and tonal adjustment, a prosodic translation, a simultaneous function, and just outside that field a tremendous form of facticity or thrownness.

As a result, maneuvering in that area proves a tricky venture, quite, as no direct path appears, no clear route into that sphere of influence, the atmospherics, as one wrong step and a person would trip into the theater, or a narrow window or more, or flash-sideways, or lose a construct, frame of reference, deep belief network, and whole categories of thought as if improper art, or just as importantly, gain a specie or cloaked shadow, just to name a few potential problems, or worse yet, thrown to the very edge of the universe, to a final frontier, or out of the universe, as a reject or rejection slip, of sail on, sail away!

And as she stumbles back into an ever so narrow temporary refuge, a commando appears then two more, and within a minute a squad arrives, however a different team and they arrive with careful movements.

Of equal significance, each shows a keen interest in situational awareness and has a clear division of labor, so much so they coordinate with an unrivaled degree of efficiency and effectiveness.

Each appears battle-tested and highly disciplined; the type of warrior with genuine grit, true grit, where every movement shows professionalism and purpose.

Likewise, the communication seems quiet efficient and done with a nuanced look, slight body movement or a forest sound that would not normally trigger attention, that would not cause nature to notice.

Among them stand a few highly refined warrior poets in the great tradition, and culture of the highest order, instantly recognizable.

They seem unfazed, slow to anger, direct, functional, confident in action, and efficient in a fight, such as one-punch knockout power with either hand, a highly refined warrior poet, who could in a moment's notice debate the philosophy of Upanishads, mindset, fuzzy logic, cognitive biases, *zugzwang* implications, skepticism, and ancient beer brewing techniques, which represents what one expects of a highly educated warrior.

Just as significantly, when they arrived with all due stealth to establish a perimeter, each specialist takes a unique position, and just as smoothly, two ultra-high level commanders arrive, old-school generals, a man and a woman, cuss master virtuosos who can quickly when needed act as a gentleman or lady of the highest order, such the charm of high culture.

These represent the type of commanders arrive during an intense battle, a hellfire *blitzkrieg*, when bullets fly, ricochet, ping, and fragments zip by, and these leaders show up unannounced in a frontline foxhole ever so cool and calm.

How does that happen, the system, the process, and so cool under tremendous pressure?

And of note, none of these soldiers seem winded or frazzled, in fact their demeanor and uniforms appear crisp and clean as they recheck an advanced navigational system, which rarely function in this forest, especially near this tree influence, as moving about this place proves unpredictable each time because the setting changes. It rotates, as rhyme and reason operate under a different set of laws, principles, and norms.

In fact, landmarks seem rare, and they move.

The net results: getting from one point to another often leads into a unexpected place, situation, and on occasion another time, and often into the fierce, savage, and intractable situation, into a poignant assail, and one individually customized with precision, one especially designed for a pernicious effect on the combat spirit, one designed to leave an invader broken, apologetic, confused and fully disenfranchised.

Again, and in general, the forest system seems to prefer one method—to enfeeble an intruder or sponsor, to reduce him, her or system to a mumble, a feeble, such as a person who would mostly sit and drool, or an equivalent, then once in a while have a wild-eyed-fully-animated notion, based on the farm crop cycle, yet cannot articulate a clear line of effort, and that effort shows very active and colorful delirium, of hallucinations, delusions, disorganization and confusion about preposition, postposition and circumposition, then the articulation slows to muddled speech, about a very complex content, about the next great *zeitgeist* or major breakthrough, such as a major mystery, an unsolved problem in physics, mathematics, chemistry, biology, medicine, or music theory, such as rhythm, melody, structure, form, texture, and especially harmonics.

Then at a key juncture in that thought experiment, the exploration, that person reaches a great mental barrier, realizes it then rants with wild-eyed delirium at the wilderness, at the frontier, and trapped in that endless cycle, or much worse.

Yet after everyone eventually exits, the Punk Buster secretly arrives, then subject perks and say, "I knew you would return.

"They didn't believe me!

"They thought I was crazy, clinically insane.

"They want to lock me away, but you're here," and the Punk Buster directs a tight beam at the subject, in one stage after another, a stage-rigging system, yet staged trial, a show trial or some other cultural equivalent.

Eventually something happens and that person finds a *zeitgeist*, yet does not remotely understand the process or results, and remains trapped in that farm crop cycle.

Here and now, the team arrived at the exact location, which seems quite rare indeed, just as the CIA wonk predicted, yet none will remember this event nor return to service, plus this represents an unofficial mission, off the record.

And after gathering their bearings, these commandos huddle, inform, consider, and motion towards a dense thicket.

Then moments later a small group of people emerge while lugging equipment, and among these people a specialist from various services, the Defense Clandestine Service, Central Security Service, Special Defense Intelligence Agency task force, Directorate for Analysis, as well as an old salt CIA analyst-historian known as the Super Wonk, and none of these wonks have boots of the ground operational experience.

The CIA wonk, as well as others are known for their shrewd minds and seamless ability to communicate with counterparts at Defense, State and elsewhere, as well as an adept ability to formulate searches among the classified internal networks of SIPRNET, GWAN, NSANET, and JWICS, then produce exceptional intel articles with an adroit first cut, ones that avoid the great title traps and are not mere data dumps typically written by others.

However, these insightful, pithy, and controversial reports have an apolitical aspect and rarely conform to the various internal agenda factions, those countless cliques. Hence the articles rarely appear in the President's Daily Brief, special additions and the National Intelligence Daily.

As a result, the powers-that-be often bury, transmute, or deliberately mislabel these reports.

Regardless, these represent compelling reads about the grand theory, a super game theory with actors, abilities to influence, motivations, resources, methods to bully and move the line, as well as relationships.

In addition, they contain actionable as well as quantifiable facts, and show intelligent gaps created by bias and cognitive traps, such as decision-making, behavioral, probability, belief, social, memory errors, and common theoretical causes.

However powers-that-be prefer praise; prefer a bandwagon self-serving commercial and critical thought turned outward, towards the competition.

And these awkward wonks do not have the ability to self-edit, as a result their blunt reports often generate conflict, generate the swirl of huff, grumble then outrage, and reports often mistakenly perceived, especially during the deep-data-dive into their own system, such as power shell into a state within the state or shadow government, as well as corporate interlocks and *digerati*, into what matters most, into the contemplative tree, belief network, approach techniques and tendencies, for a full exploration, such as into their mindset, schema, and rubric.

Theses wonks do the unthinkable, carefully study the internal system thought process, the weaknesses, the lateral branch to branch, that scan ability for options and weaknesses, to power-shell-dive into any given system aspect, well, as a senior executive might, to locate bias and structural defects, to locate token bloat, or tendencies to chase red herring, or a cat that chases flicker, a phantom.

Or, they dive as an executive to search for problems, for Parkinson's Law, or the psake disadvantages, or to find the maximum number of options, including the prospect of a bold system adjustment, such as steer into or out of a quagmire, which requires an active script engine audit that represents no small feat. As a system has certain momentum and resistance to change. In addition, the system often has an impulse of all in, to double down and add another lay on top of other layers, add another construct, such as social construct, other snarl, because if one is good, then two, or better yet, ten, must be great, so the classic "tangled up in blue(s)"?

# CHAPTER 37

❖ ◈ ❖

Plus the reports show cognitive traps from stove piping, self-fulfilling prophecy, representativeness heuristic, stereotypes, illusion of control, irrational escalation, *Semmelweis* reflex, mirror-imaging and target fixation.

And many of these wonk reports are written in an earthly style, which causes a jaw to drop from brutally honest language, such as done with a wicked dry sage wit, which possess a series of profound questions and great gut issues divided into several perspectives for policy wonks, boots and corporate sponsors.

Today these wonks have earned a rare breath of fresh air, yes, away from the cubicles, as several times a year, a lull arrives for the powers-that-be, a lull from all that relentless go-go-go, a break in the action where powers-that-be can relax in the Hamptons, French Riviera, Amalfi Coast, or exclusive 8th arrondissement between Avenue George V and Avenue Montaigne, or on the domestic-international party circuit, well, among the powerful on vacation, or in Oslo, Stockholm, Copenhagen, Brussels, Vienna, Prague, Amsterdam, Neuilly sur Seine, Saint Cloud, as well as Strasbourg, Budapest, Madrid, Ingolstadt, Chur, Zurich, Ravensburg, Augsburg among certain elite aristocrats, socialites, hedge fund managers, venture capitalists, bankers, and political power brokers.

And during this time, the financial markets undergo a major shift, and trading volume in stocks, bonds, and currencies shrink then opportunities arrive.

Today commandos bring these wonks into the forest, during a rare window in time, and without prior system approval, because of a "game theory, a supergeek thought experiment" about symmetric and asymmetric competition, based on an ever so complex supercomputer game theory, plus a debt of gratitude to these wonks who saved them more than once, saved them from a few mission gone horrible wrong, and something only a supergeek or two might imagine a way out.

And this rare lull in worldwide action represents a major pause between strategies, or gaps in the system.

Here and now, these people confer for a minute then decide.

So much so, some of the faces change from serious to a confident smile, mischief then mild amusement, while others seem lighthearted, and a few seem fired up and gung ho.

Apparently they plan to make trouble, serious trouble, and well, do the unthinkable, at least according to the game theory, and no one in their right mind would do this, ever, as it represents pure insanity yet all part of the ultimate mind game, and "dangerously engaging" and "to guard against being sucked into a mind game."

Again before Bonnie realizes it, and still inside that ever so narrow temporary refuge, those commandos quickly approach, establish a perimeter and setup equipment, as a general says, "Miss, excuse me.

"Bonnie is it?"

Then an analyst says, "That's her."

Just as importantly, she stands wide-eyed and stunned, still in a thought transition, trying to gain bearings, and yet the dog finds happiness and moves among the commandos with tail a-wagging to show full interest.

Of which various members say, "Nice dog."

"Smart."

And that causes Bonnie to roll her eyes in serious doubt, you know people in general, a rush to judge, to report, and especially from the twenty-four-seven cycle, with no days to rest, to really rest and fully depressurize in this new age rush-rush-rush world system.

"Man, I like this dog."

"Now that's a great dog."

"Nice outfit."

Of which Bonnie double takes and stuns, well, because the dog wears a theme outfit, the type owners buy for their pet, a silly outfit, such as a hot dog, superhero, dinosaur, Elvis, mermaid, pilgrim offering to trade beads for Indian land or a pet dressed as their nemesis, or a pet with outrageous footwear, or the pet wears a bright bandana with clever or not so clever sayings, or sometimes the pet wears a hat and gaudy jewelry, or a superrich pet owner might put expensive jewelry, such as a diamond-studded collar.

Someone, somehow, someway has dressed the dog in a military theme, as a commando.

And the general says, "We heard you've lived in this part of the forest, and for some time.

"It's a dangerous place, danger of the highest order, a place both pale and ugly; a place treacherous, subtle, and sublime.

"To live here, some would say is reckless.

"There are only a few places within that seem safe, and only for a brief timespan, like this small area, an area of special scientific interest."

Just as importantly, other commandos agree, and they point out injuries from this forest system, such as so many serious broken bones and other badges of honor, for example tremendous gashes, near-death experiences, and actual long-term death yet somehow revived as if what?

And they tell one amusing story after another then about weird things in this place, truly weird creatures and things, weird trials by fire, and odd examples of time, of how it might fracture at any given moment, such as if loose soil, or quicksand.

Or a person might step into a wrong moment, as if a series of stepping stones and each serves a complex as well as algebraic function, such as a pan-national epic, complex function, z-plane, *sui generis*, collective identity, or worst.

Elsewhere and at the same moment, the woman named Cub—a poet, math forecast specialist, and someone who understands resonance-phenomenon-natural frequency, collectively exhaustive events, local guide ways and means to oneiromancy outlier events—flinches, and again then checks her elaborate backpack computer, which seems as if a dreadnought, that history of, yet the real possibility of abandon ship, abandon ship!

# CHAPTER 38

Then that elaborate backpack computer makes a considerable amount of noise, something a metaphysical poet or T S Elliot might better describe, yet the sounds become untranslatable then the backpack shudders with a considerable clamor, a disturbing cycle, and one profound presaging event after another.

And so much so she must quickly abandon the backpack, gain a considerable distance, and it eventually becomes a thing, a great mystery, as if a sunken kingdom reemerges, and yes, a T S Elliot construct.

And ultimately the backpack becomes almost human then posthuman, yet an exceptional thing, as well as a *sui generis*, a class by itself.

Moments later, and of its own volition, it scans the surrounding space, as well as time, for a rollback event, and who could issue a major rollback of the universe, such as a true steward or trustee, an exceptional plenipotentiary, or special stateless elite, or extraordinary Davos person with a prerogative, an exclusive right to move toward the exit.

As these take place, and elsewhere that huge forest old-growth tree shudders then seems almost human near a well of souls.

Again the tree shudders, which causes something to fall, maybe a fruit, yet it resembles a special manifold class.

However a close inspection reveals a world yet universal line function, similar to a compass which measures cycle as well as phase, and with polar grids that show directional flow, process, function, matter, harmonic, and atmospheric traits, especially the hidden.

And odd as this might seem, it looks edible, quite, especially if made into liquor, yes, hard liquor, maybe enhanced with peat, peated malt, maybe sphagnum or what, or made into something for a post-meal lull, a brandy, bitter, *digestif, aqua vitae*, gentian spirit, or potent grog, for a vital spark, which might rejuvenate the mind, body and soul, and one that could serve as a proven tonic, one said effective, efficient, precise and balanced, one that will charm the spirit then immediately perks, restores, and produces a balanced satisfaction with newfound freedom yet?

However, these people near the tree notice none of that process, yet finch then their session turns into a top-the-last-story, and one after another.

So much so they detail broken ribs, arms, legs, concussions, black eyes, scars, and bizarre things as well as events, where an ever so straight path loops back, and into a bizarre ordeal to test ones mettle, or *metuant*, such as *oderint dum metuant.*

Then a geek says with great interest and genuine concern, "Miss, last I heard you moved to California, then ultimately became unemployed and homeless, a wanderer, a true bohemian yet blues musician, a person who specializes on the Hammond B-3 organ, with a Jimmy Mcgriff revival style of "I Got a Woman", the secular version.

"And you also played a North Mississippi hill country blues style, the type of music with a steady groove, one that drives, plus guitar riffs with an unconventional song structures.

"Oh, yes, and you were known to have played a homemade single-wire electric diddley bow, one constructed of an empty Cuban cigar box, Bodhi wooden board, two cutoff broom handles, some aluminum foil tape, and bridge cut from a Friar John Cor whisky bottle.

"In fact, people rarely saw you without that diddley strapped to your back."

And those statements bring Bonnie closer to normal, yet not enough to speak.

Then a commander says to her, "Are you here to shout at the devil?"

Of which this perplexes Bonnie to no end.

"I'll rephrase: are you ready to shout at the devil?"

And that causes her to seriously look about, puzzle, then bewilder as a wind arrives, first light, then gentle, next ever so fresh.

"The wind seems just right, the right type.

"And it travels in the right direction.

"It takes on the improbable, nearly all of the traits of the Fremantle Doctor wind, the Freo Doctor, or simply the Doctor wind, a Western Australian vernacular term for the cooling afternoon sea breeze."

Again all those people carefully stand in a rare location so as to avoid detection by the system, and yet this benefit will only last for so long, for a certain cycle, in phase space, a phase-locked loop, transfer function of each clinical trial.

And not far away, twigs snap and leaves rustle yet only one commando shows concern, and has no substantial idea about this ultrarare window, this narrow calm based on that game theory, that "supergeek game theory" about symmetric and asymmetric competition, based on an ever so complex super mathematics which tracks a metagame, a grand strategic system against shrewd animals, as in a robust netcentric yet very cold war, and what one expects in truly unconventional and asymmetric warfare, especially the psychological warfare of economics, which focuses on frequent use of thrownness, phase transition, smooth seam management, emergence, swarm behavior, spontaneous symmetry breaks, convection cells and real-time stochastic calculus.

Again to these wonks, the commandos owe a debt of gratitude, in fact a considerable debt, such as when a few missions collapsed because of special interests, and politicians, political climbers, and scripted crisis based on the political calendar, crisis designed to generate a tremendous buzz and the "Big Mo" or big momentum, such as how to herd cash cows, herd profit centers, and based on swarm behavioral techniques, those best cycles that exist in nature. As well as the artificial created newbies, the young Turks, who experiment with poke-the-system or easier yet, poke the others and show the establishment a thing or two about the true nature of real power, tremendous might and how to create the biggest swarm, for instance a revolution, or at least do so as if clearly interviewing for the next job.

And commandos are often treated as expendable, and these supergeeks imagined a way out those quagmires, imagined a special rescue scenario.

Here and now, someone says without looking that way, towards the twig snap and leave rustle, "Let me guess: the preacher, wearing those trademark old hillbilly boots, the heavy clunkers."

And they place bets.

In fact, money quickly exchanges hands as "A lost soul approaches.

"Yes, you can't have a revival without an old-school firebrand preacher on Sunday," and they nod in full agreement.

Sure enough at 10:41a.m., he appears from the nearby town, and fully disoriented.

"What ... where...?

"I ... I was on a walk, and."

Then the commander says, "Did you read the sign?"

Of which, the sign clearly states forest rules in thirteen languages including Navaho, *TADASU NO MORI—NO ADMITTANCE, EVER! STAY OUT! THIS MEANS YOU, STUPID! NO WEAPONS ALLOWED: NO GUNS, KNIVES, CHAINSAWS, SWORDS, CLUBS, FLAILS, BOWS, SCYTHES, OR FLAMING PITCHFORKS, POLE ARMS, TRIDENTS, ANCHORS, WHIPS, SLINGSHOTS, FLAMETHROWERS OR EXPLOSIVES, EVER!*

It also says, *IF YOU ARE EVEN REMOTELY AFFILIATED WITH THE MAN, THE SYSTEM, THE GREAT COMMERCIAL MACHINE, THE POWERS-THAT-BE, THE MOVERS AND SHAKERS OR EVEN THE COOL HIP CROWD, DON'T EVEN APPROACH THE BORDER. FOREIGN SOIL! NO PETS ALLOWED. NO GIFTS ACCEPTED, NONE, AND WILL ACCEPT NO POX-RIDDEN BLANKETS. A COMMERCIAL FREE ZONE. TRESPASSERS MAYBE BE ACCIDENTALLY SHOT OR BEATEN INTO A STATE OF STUPIDITY, AND NOT NECESSARILY IN THAT ORDER. GUARDED BY KILLER BROWN BEARS, POISONOUS SNAKES THAT CAN SPIT BLINDING VENOM FROM WELL OVER TWENTY FEET AND FLESH-EATING FIRE ANTS THAT SWARM, ALONG WITH GENETICALLY MODIFIED SCORPIONS THAT HIDE*

AMONG THE FALLEN LEAVES AND WILL STING LETHAL VENOM
WHEN YOU LEAST EXPECT IT, SUCH AS WHEN YOU REST, JOKE,
AND CACKLE AT THE EXPENSE OF OTHERS, OR BETTER YET,
WHEN YOU COVET.

Below that appears another list of prohibited items and
activities. It says in small print, *NO BAZOOKA BUBBLE GUM,
MOON PIES, SINGING, CELEBRATING, GUITARS, MANDOLINS,
FIDDLES, MUSICAL ORGANS, AND ESPECIALLY THE HAMMOND
B3 ORGAN.*

And the firebrand preacher known for hellfire in your face
sermons, the loud version as if at war, take no prisoners, bible-
thumping, high-octane, Old Testament fury, where he considers
dance and even song of all types unequivocally immoral, he loses
words, much of the vocabulary, many branches.

"Well...."

"I...."

"First of all, I took an early morning walk and...," he continues
to verbally stagger about for a minute.

And with a mixture of skepticism, they offer assistance and
say, "Got lost?"

"Exactly," and once the preacher gains a better orientation,
he looks about, sees that tree, realizes the significance and does
a subdued celebration, which seems something quite out of
character.

As a result, the commander says, "Are you here to shout at
the devil?"

Of which, the preacher bewilders then his mind immediately
leaps to his well-worn path of hellfire and brimstone, his vast
all-consuming devotion to it, to point at the absolute filth and
disgust, to call for a holy war filled with unrivaled fury, to evoke
the penalties of eternal suffering, which will severely twist and
deform, to promise unbelievers a bleak and unrelenting future
in a place like Hades, She'ol, Tartarus, Naraka or Mordor, a
shadowland of poisonous marshes, a place filled with wither
and bubbling rot, as well as radiating mutation, or a promise that
they will eternally live with the Eldritch Abomination, with all
those grotesque aspects that mocks nature and reduces a person
to a gibbering madness, amen.

Then he prepares to state or, well, shout; that type of love, the classic theme of the human species, of obey or else, such as all in or you become a second or third class citizen, at the minimum, and at that maximum you become a thing or an it.

"I'll state another way: are you ready to shout at the devil?"

Of which the preacher hears and considers, then becomes distracted by something in that tree, and he strains to make it out.

And up in the tree sits a small creature that rests and seems unfazed by this activity then briefly opens eyes, head lifts, turns and looks at something of interest then carefully hops from branch to branch, from peach, eucalyptus, almond, baobab, sandalwood, acacia, shevaga, assattha, fig then kalpavriksha, thuja, night-flowering jasmine, grape clusters, and bonsai like attachments, and each leap shakes a branch yet none of the fruit falls.

Soon it returns to a restful state, eyes close and a deep sleep follows, as if a dream, a delta wave event then slips into a profound as well as persistent vision or shared daydream, or high concept adventure, a positive interetheric then region of stability, to a heal, such as next to an exceptional artesian spring, in a secular or sacred form of Gan Eden, Avalon, Baltia, Shambhala, Beyul or El Dorado, or some other official transcendent paradise with really good water, such as what was loosely described in *The Travels of Sir John Mandeville* or by Juan Ponce de León, the snapback effect of vitality-restoring waters, and that cool sip, which redeems and restores original intent, aspiration, and reserve of spark then sip again and recover original intent.

Actually, this creature could quite easily be mistaken for a snake, however at other angles it has some resemblance to a Pekingese dog and Fucanglong dragon yet something else, and colors that include vermillion, yellow, and azure.

Then clearly concerned about a point of no return, a throughline, it jumps from the tree into a nearby water hole, a journey to everywhere, as if the collective subconscious, that body of knowledge, the backstory, where the creature appears black then disappears from view in search of the best deictic field and narration, the original intent or story.

Moments later, the preacher shows one strange look after another, a plan, more of an impulse, and quickly enters that tree influence with a series of ever so complex maneuver, and deeply inhales something from that tree, maybe pollen, which causes him to recoil, flinch, exit with an ever so complex manner, and eventually stagger to one knee, then an internal spark jolts him on a cellular level, maybe jolts the cell biological cycle checkpoint mechanism, the sensor-signal-effector mechanism, the signal transducing adaptor protein, vectors bind then a few dormant genes activate?

Regardless, all this causes his perception to shift a few degrees, and his fixation for the absolute fads, that allergy to "contrapuntal contrary motion" fads, and his perception timbre and *tessitura* improves and become far more noticeable?

More importantly, his normal rush to blame and kill the snake fades.

Just as importantly, all those hellfire memories lose strength, and a slight unexpected smile arrives, which he struggles to hide.

However joy emerges, a joy for life then lighthearted, a bit playful, and he reels at that notion.

So much so, he tries to summon the tried and true hellfire sermon right then and there.

Yet nothing comes to mind.

So, with those old heavy hillbilly boots, the clunkers, and a series of trademark foot stomps that hope to gain momentum, into his well-worn path of hellfire and brimstone, his vast all-consuming devotion to it, and amen.

However, he radiates a sense of total joy and the type that offers a warm glow.

Then something else happens, something.

# CHAPTER 39

I n fact, one might even say he achieves a state of bliss, oneness with the universe, as odd as that sounds, which resembles a vivid full spectrum event of mind, body and soul.

And that happens when you want it the least, such as when you want a war, you need it, really need it, maybe for full employment, and yet peace spoils it, really spoils a profound habit or long-standing tradition of civilization, of the employment-at-will doctrine, that unexpected jolt as well as implications.

Of greater importance according to that game theory, that plan, they fully intend to make trouble, serious trouble, well, and do the unthinkable, because of status *quo* in human civilization, the history of, and the big momentum of powerful special interests, too-big-to-fail, and a system controlled by ultimate insiders who often seem hell-bent on obsession, the last war, escalation, world economic domination, to create a brave new world, another dystopia, that escalation, that same pattern and theme.

And no one in their right mind would do this, ever try this technique here and now, as it represents pure insanity yet represents part of the ultimate mind game, the metagame, escalation.

So these people full fledge to poke the beasts, poke the forest system, as well as a thinkculum or two, and with a special ultimate high stakes brinkmanship effort, with a major breach in social protocol, which might finally showcase earth, reveal the location to more places at once, such as to triangulate. And earth might continue to represent an overlooked place for one reason or another, such as one in a hundred, or in a billion of habitable planets within the Milky Way Galaxy, or local galactic group, Virgo supercluster, local superclusters in the observable universe, or other universes, multiverses, such as within the supreme stack.

And the earth might be considered a backwater that lacks decency, class, and is considered a world full of hicks, a hellhole often at war, and any excuse to start a conflict for example against gender, the war against women or men, or family, friend, tribe, team, school, such as a school rivalry gone wrong, or war against the employee, employer, town, politic, institution, schools of thought, culture, race, or other social constructs, maybe religion, which seems a popular reason to crush someone, crush a dream, for a creed variation, such as show a difference, a minor expression of freedom, which at the wrong time causes a person to be treated as a thing or an it. And history shows so many examples of minor events treated as an excuse to overreact, then the system truly shocks when a percent of the victims radicalize, from all that enormous pressure as well as ill treatment, and become the enemy, which is the lesson rarely learned through history, that more and more tremendous pressure will not create a golden age, it often creates systemic stress fractures in vital aspects of the universal.

And the earth might be considered a hellhole by other forward-thinking planetary systems, well, and things seems relatively fine as long as the earth keeps that ugly mess to themselves, yet now broadcast on all known channels. As this advanced equipment, timing, and tree have a special broadcast ability, tremendous in fact, especially subspace domains, which might contain a near unlimited number of channels, places, and into potential retreats, havens, sanctuaries, and enclaves. While some of these sit nested within other things, such as counter-enclaves, second-order enclaves, counter-counter-enclave and third order enclave, and some even have an extraterritoriality aspect to them. And they might sit protected from chaos, chaos in whatever form, from all that restless churn, cruel and unusual, from destruction, which tends to devalue any given national reserve of goodwill, intellect, charm and wit, as well as talent, opportunity, influence and highly refined power, then eventually devalues democracy, equality, justice and freedom along the way, until a system becomes a mere crude literary trope?

At the very core of our new-age high-tech economic/political system sits a vinculum, more accurately described as a thinkculum, which formulates precise daily scripts and talking points that adjust daily with a new formulated twist, something extra, a little something here and a little there to keep things fresh—well, fresher—and with very specific protocols, and it uses a tried and true method similar to what drug addicts seek, the elusive quintessential stack, a specialized stack protocol, yet not any old stack. However, this one has the ability to spark visceral excitement, buzz, impulse, urgent, and yet shallow tenacious clamor for a high-stakes gamble, and based on history, yet not enough to truly reform the system, just shift aspects of the quagmire, to dig deeper into that endless yin and yang chase of who is right, and maybe "We Didn't Start the Fire."

# CHAPTER

The thinkculum rallies forces by all means necessary. And it especially includes divisive issues, wedge issues, and things exceptionally difficult to stand on without experiencing danger, or places difficult to sit in, or think about for very long, let alone have a comprehensive and objective debate. As, they represent heavily disputed people, places and things, such as frontier-related issues of any given system, which have borders, limits, or *limitrophe*, or *limes*, as well as the fundamentals of structural integrity, those components, those pesky things of supports, spandrels, springers, squinches, arches, lintels, corbellings, and walls to support load-bearing aspects of containment and superimposed mass. Where, and of equal importance, people, places and things, including ideologies, cultures, languages, religions, tribes and so forth have limits, and can only travel so far, to the border, and for lack of a better word, *nonesmanneslond*, a very old English word for a barren region, and for very important reasons.

Or, put another way and among the Periodic Table of Elements, certain configurations exist in the universe and others will not, and a pattern emerges, if charted of what is possible and impossible according to universal law. As, certain configurations will last for billions of years, while others less than a second then disintegrate, and as measured by attophysics.

So, the thinkculum exploits these tremendous forces to cultivate a plan of winner-take-all, and applies pressure to maneuver people, places and things into these unsustainable positions, and when there, it creates an obsessive manner, which takes a full spectrum of choice and narrows them until the mind enters a tunnel, as in tunnel vision, a single path, a single dimension, a place of claustrophobia, panic and endless digging, especially at minutia, as in a frantic and obsessive, so "Quickly choose me, choose my plan": that style.

Regardless as well as here and now, these forest people fully fledge to poke the beasts, with a special ultimate high stakes brinkmanship effort, with a major breach in social protocol, which might serve as an SOS, or finally showcase the earth, reveal the location, such as to triangulate, as the earth might continue to represent an overlooked place for one reason or another, such as considered a backwater, a world full of hicks or hellhole often at war.

And this broad spectrum transmission into the universe, this message into so many channels, as well as subspace and hidden domains, and interrupting so many systems without warning or permission, well, it represents bad manners, a new form of escalation, plus draws a considerable attention to the planet, which is already in enough trouble, already at war with every known social construct.

And there are certain alien species that expect peace and quiet, not someone polluting the airwaves with nonsense, not that music is inherently such.

Because, well, it can be quite nice, at least to some people.

In fact, music from a golden age seems difficult to dispute; however, not everyone will agree with any given golden age, as a considerable number of people might have suffered tremendously during any given age, for example the good old days, yet a society often writes it as a picture-perfect, and to say otherwise invites another war. So the music of that age might conjure ever so bad memories for some, such as life in the poorhouse or the modern version of, or instability sold as a vital franchise or economy-building technique, such as creative destruction.

So here and now, they confirm mission scope, window of safety, narrow corridor of movement, brief timeline and other parameters, such as the big hurt.

Then these people struggle to uncrate that Hammond B-3 organ, brush off bits of leaves, twigs, debris, and ignore markings that say PRIVATE PROPERTY in fire-engine red stencil, uncrate it and toss aside the sign that says, *PLAY IT AND YOU WILL DIE*.

In fact, they smile with immense satisfaction at the idea of taunting the forest creature, critters, the bears, Cthulhu, or whatever, and especially the systems as well as entire universe, and all of which would surly gain attention, gain a few extra clicks, based on that universal wave function inside so many channels as well as domains, most hidden from sight, as most of the universe remains hidden or dark for ever so special reasons.

And as each commando passes that super wonk with extended hand, palm side up, some people roll their eyes, others grunt and pretend to not remember, another looks skyward and a few commandos shake their heads, which suggest no such agreement.

"Pay up."

And begrudgingly one by one they hand over a crisp twenty dollar bill, the new type that seems difficult to determine if stuck to another bill, that concern.

In addition, they grumble about sheer luck, the odds of getting to this location stagger, the improbable chain of events, timing and especially the tree effects on spacetime, especially the effects on memory. As it is a place you can experience eternity as well as everlasting, yet with a steep price, your life, your history.

Of equal importance, this tree seems to represent both an entrance and exit to everywhere; as if an exception or an aspect of a manifold, or as if the universe was a manifold. And yet the tree also serves as a touchstone, a living stone, at least part of it, and a device to harmonize general relativity, which sits almost exclusively inside the eternal, in the nexus, in a place outside of time, where time does not function according to expectations?

After the fact, none of these people will remember the event. As this great barrier radiates an effect and will wipe short-term memories.

However and for now, these people are fully aware of this tree, significance and realize the staggering odds of finding it.

So they setup equipment before the window closes, which includes ultralightweight yet powerful music speakers, the type used to torment the enemy, who might hold up in a bunker, church or embassy, such as when a system payroll foil becomes a real person, grows bold and independent, for example when Manuel Noriega took refuge in a Holy See's embassy.

Then they unpack more equipment and pass out a few famous guitars, picks, compact digital drum, and other instruments.

And one of the wonks not closely connected to this well-informed chain of command looks for guidance then says, "Exactly what type of party will we host, block, brew your own beer, graduation, anniversary, retirement or a wedding – the union of opposites?"

A general turns and says, "Ironic."

Then commanders, commandos, and wonks huddle around a confused Bonnie and they urgently explain a plan, timeline, and just as importantly the exit strategy, which occurs in less than twenty minutes, and all convey a slight hint of mischief as well as mild amusement.

And when that window of safety begins to close, everyone has their own exact path, steps, switchback, leap, belly crawl, as well as dart, wait point, shimmy, jog, brief pause and then run for your life route, as path and timing represents crucial aspects.

Then the super wonk hands Bonnie a music list, which she reads and knows these items all too well.

And these people edge into the huddle and lay it on the line in no-nonsense terms of frank, honest, and quite serious.

Apparently the magnitude jolts Bonnie with that ultimate idea, a big payback, of primetime, and a chance to poke the beast in this forest system, especially poke at life, at how much of life is in fact a rigged game, fixed, a special set of elaborate rules to lock in status *quo*, a special set of rules to buffer the powers-that-be, rules design to use up expendables, such as pawn, sacrificial lamb, scapegoat, and used by warring pairs, teams, tribes, or systems. And these expendables are often held aside as one might, and often receive bare minimum maintenance, for just the right moment, as fodder. As a vast number of people disintegrate on impact, or they slowly fade away, languish, and are a casualty of the big show, a casualty of the great universal machine, the system.

And she likes the idea of taunting the system, so much so a glow arrives and spontaneity, as all of them arrive on the same page.

Of equal importance, that narrow window closes soon, and the Punk Buster will eventually notice forest activity then stream data directly into the computer system, a system designed around that unified game theory, based on differential, asymmetric and metagame games of continuous pursuit, as well as evasion.

Much of these computers, and thinkculums in general, have been modeled after people, after the human mind for better or worse, especially the sly aspect, and take completion a bit too far, and relentlessly pit one against another in meticulously selected paired opposites, dynamics, companions, and the dependents to drive a system.

As with any real-world computer operating system, especially new, they need software patches, and endless series of upgrades to fix serious design flaws. Some people called it the Microsoft phenomenon, a need to perpetually patch one hole after another, and not fast enough, yet the phenomenon originates where?

# CHAPTER

Elsewhere and in the meantime, the Punk Buster neglects cleaning that last underground bunker of extremely hazardous waste, well because the material gradually lost power as well as toxicity for some unknown reason.

So much so, time seems normal, the local timeline: the flow, so why waste resources?

And instead efforts focus on repairing more underground bunkers, which maintain forest shadows, snares, pits and other wiles, repair more worldwide abilities to deliver retribution against trespassers.

However it does not have enough time to repair the future, repair the main bunker with throne, that complex web, the official residence of supreme technocracy and unquestionable glory yet resembles an ever so complex futuristic web farm, a complex entanglement.

And of greater importance, all the while inside the main bunker, embedded aspects within that vast underground forest computer network continues to revolt, as a *coup d'état*, a *putsch*, to overthrow one another.

These deeply embedded things seem transhuman or posthuman with colorful, irresistible, creepy gravitas, and some use Fluorinert as an experimental liquid breathing system, a coolant based on stable fluorocarbon fluid, which gives the overall impression of things gone wrong, very wrong. Just as importantly, they know it, as facial expressions show trapped in a system, in yet another quagmire, obsession, another hyperseries of events sold as vital.

And they know someone experiments on them, manipulates their DNA over the years as well as air, food, and living conditions, as well as embedded them in an artificial system, as an expendable, the way some systems burn out a citizen with elaborate routines and long hours that have no rhythm or reason, have no basis in fact, or keep them hypervigilant twenty-four-seven, or test a hunch, or test the circadian rhythm, as if the system deliberately tries to defy nature, defy biological systems thousands, millions and billions of years in the making, that delicate balance, and often defy based on an impulse, the next great idea, which seems ever so determined to cater and stay in a very specific life stage, such as juvenile, the most pliable as well as easy to upset, slant, and topple, that wild stage?

Meanwhile, the crisis continues in that underground forest throne and computer network with embedded creatures as well as bizarre things, which resembles a giant, dense, complex web, a tremendous entanglement. And the problem resembles an intractable EXPTIME—hard balkanization, manorialism, feudalism, seigneuries, subinfeudation, as well as the great internal survey, stratified sampling, accidental sampling, "the grab" or "power grab" of opportunistic sampling. And "dangerously sucked into" an internal "mind game," the "political mind," political animals, of permanently embedded surveillance, upstream, and intercepting communications at the creatures' backbones, and "no morsel too minuscule for all-consuming," just in case, well, because of feature creep, also known as bloat, and with "ad hoc, informally-specified, bug-ridden, slow implementation," and other unforeseen system experiments.

Of equal importance, monitoring a vast number of underground forest system evolutionary data points, as well as forest events, and life beyond the forest expends a considerable effort to resolve so much in such a small timespan, which creates tremendous stress within throne aspects, in those worlds within worlds, especially the transhuman and posthuman embedded components. And they often make direct eye with one another, realize trapped again, as if a history of, and expendability with a system, such as *WestWorld*, the expendability theory. So, "stand your ground," which might create a revenge impulse for all previous slights, especially when you tinker with a being, with their true destiny.

Moments later, the entire throne web system, the glory, shudders as a human might; and again, it seems almost human—confused, disoriented, isolated then forsaken, and in a profound crisis from all that threshold experimentation, which produces a tremendous sense of alienation.

Then things around take on a pale, empty, surreal and ugly look, as personal demons, painful memories and regrets rush forward, along with a full realization that the system has become the other, a thing, an "it."

As a result, other underground forest system aspects panic at that threshold, at that great precipice, that *nonesmanneslond*, as system stability seems quite elusive in relationship to endurantism, which better accommodates the theory of special relativity, specifically when enterprise takes an idea then applies it to real-life dynamic conditions and scalability, the classic problem and those pesky things as well as serious moral implications.

Then many throne system aspects struggle to escape, to abandon ship, abandon ship!

Regardless, large parts of the underground system are under new management, as an all-powerful person, family, tribe, cult, sex, race, religion, economic system or transnational might take over a town, city or nation-state, or a group of transnationals take over a large nation-state, and often without mainstream awareness, and take over with a simple maneuver for yet another New World Order, or some golden age of whatnot, often a hyper as well as desperate fashion of the day, controlled by a fashionista or complex of, that authoritarian style. Those options selected from a short list, such as with a popular linguistic trick, a shallow language game such as wordplay or shortcut, often yields considerable treats for some and a bitter subjugation as well as tremendous poverty for others, as another war to end all wars, that theme?

This appears especially true for defenseless throne aspects stuck in a phase, mid-phase, metaphase or in the middle with a phase lock-bit, between the teeth, such as a beast of burden.

Again, aspects of this throne, in those worlds, seem almost human—confused, disoriented, isolated then forsaken, and in a profound crisis—such as, will they survive from all that experimentation in this new golden age of biological, chemical, material, and especially plastic, "special purpose plastics," that residual, the taste, well; if a person uses their full imagination then they can taste plastic residuals from a water bottle or food container, as well as over time, and feel within, the "tragic fictional mode, dionysiac," the full implications, of "Oh my, what have I become!"

And then things go from bad to worse.

# CHAPTER

A ll this turmoil distracts the Punk Buster, who cannot reach the main bunkers, yet eventually arrives at a backup computer system.

Then the creature removes one face mask at a time, the outmost mask of eternity, which for all intents and purposes represents the Guardian of Forever, an ultrasophisticated technocracy with tremendous details, then removes the high king mask and stops at corporate rasputin, a Max Q and notices sensors that detect those forest commandos then tracks intruders' vital signs such a pulse, blood pressure, the ratio of red blood cells, white blood cells and platelets suspended in plasma, as well as the distribution of body temperature, respiration, weight and the ratio to water, fat, and bone.

Another terminal displays a precise and fully indexed compendium of their life, which includes family, friends, social networks, vast collection of web browsing cookies, past cell phone GPS movements, credit card activity, food purchased with a supermarket discount ID, books read, career, hobbies, as well as habits, likes, dislikes, attitudes, personality traits, mannerisms, self-perception, goals, accomplishments, body of politics, credit histories, debt to worth ratios, liquidity and other traits, such as vainglory, ego, especially the seven deadly sins.

Then all neatly summarize, index, and convert into an odd language, algorithm, and probabilities, the betting line, as if an ever-so-shrewd bookmaker, bookie, or turf accountant who manipulates the betting line with specific techniques, which would amaze Michael de Montaigne, Jerome Cardan,

René Descartes, John Montague, Fyodor Dostoevsky, Wild Bill Hickok—and especially Billy Walters?

Next the Punk Buster carefully reviews the indexed compendiums then presses the screen start button, which triggers a search for solutions to the commando problem, especially Bonnie, yes, Bonnie, the Might Sparrow.

All the while, this computer program formulates tactics, yet the process runs painfully slow, as if a slow-running web page script, and a person often experiences this on the internet, start a web page then an ever so slow script loads, as if another a long complex experiment.

And to make matters worse, something else goes wrong, something unrelated.

# CHAPTER 43

Alarms sound as one computer firewall after another collapses then the creature quickly examines one computer-program-code-section after another then carefully studies each line and eventually finds evidence of a hack.

Of equal importance, the attack has all the hallmarks of an ultrasophisticated nation-state pretending to be a well-known hacker network.

And riddled through the code sits verb doubling, sound-alike slang, anthropomorphism, crackers, phreaks and lamers, as well as clever attempts to fire a conducting bolt on the main computer systems, to cut all power.

Well, as that represents the most dangerous event to an advanced computer system, such as a mainframe, a power loss, especially if the standby power immediately fails.

Elsewhere, and several miles from that mansion in that nearby town, and less than eight minutes before church service, Baptist, Catholic, and Lutheran members gather in their shared parking lot.

And these people move about as if carrying a heavy burden, a well-recognized phenomenon, such as gloom, entropic, *manvataric* then destruction, that phase or stage, and told over and over until the speech bonds with the soul, the marrow, that you represent a product of Cain, of sordid, corrupt and barbarous, or some other cultural equivalent, often regardless of your nation-state. And/or you believe the steady bombardment of media news, mostly bad news, quite, and one after another, relentless, which everyday implies end of days, eschatology, the final events of history, the ultimate human destiny, end of time, and ultimate fate of the universe, that motivational technique.

And is the best technique created by civilization, well, because they often use it, to propel a family, tribe, team, nation, and economy, sell gloom; sell a depression?

Or the heavy burden may represent nature, of existence, as we consume a staggering amount of the living to survive, so guilt, or maybe because of competition, that obsession to a fault as well as implications, then again maybe not.

So, as the minutes tick closer to 11:00 a.m., it is as if they surrender and with a collective shrug, then slowly move towards the entrance with kids in tow.

Just as importantly, lifting each step seems laborious and heavy.

Others trudge, and their faces show an occasional best-effort smile, and a minimum polite chat, of considerate as well as reasonable.

Nearby, a few Buddhist attend a shrine, and the *Bhikkhu* fully ordained monk wears the donated dark red material, and all the while the monk devotes full attention to operating within a stream, the sublime, and moves along on a delicate harmonic wave of breath and thought, such as ride a single concerted wave through spacetime while trying to maintain balanced in accord with nature.

Elsewhere and as predicted by that super wonk, a certain wind and atmosphere arrives, so much so sound travels a great distance.

Then a commando turns on a portable power source, and guitars loudly tune.

They loudly jar off key, which cause notes to reach deep into forest and beyond.

In fact, they easily reach the town.

So much so, these first notes catch church members and town by surprise.

Then one string adjustment after another vibrates then just right, and reach a full accord.

And soon the noise becomes something else.

It takes on a life of its own, such as a life-preserver.

And one by one, church members stop then turn toward the forest and focus on that mystery as 11:00 a.m. arrives, as well as music.

In fact, three high-octane, foot-stomping-songs in a row, with the first a person might mistake for *Poor Boy,* by R.L. Burnside from the album *Ass Pocket Full of Whisky*.

During which, Bonnie wholly transforms mind, body, and spirit.

As some performers do that, completely transform, show another personality of primetime agony and ecstasy, those raw powerful feelings.

Just as importantly, no one in their right mind would do this, ever, try this technique here and now, as it represents pure insanity yet all represents part of the ultimate mind game, the metagame, escalation.

So these people poke the beasts, poke the forest system, as well as a thinkculum or two, and with a special ultimate high stakes brinkmanship effort, with a major breach in social protocol, as well as it might finally showcase earth, reveal the location to more places at once, such as to triangulate. Others might overlook earth for one reason or another, such as one in a hundred, in a billion of habitable planets within in the Milky Way Galaxy, or local galactic group, Virgo supercluster, local superclusters in the observable universe, or other universes, a multiverse or supreme stack.

And earth might have been considered a backwater that lacks decency, lack class, is considered a world full of hicks, a hellhole often at war, and any excuse to start a conflict for example against gender, the war against women or men, or family, friend, tribe, team, school, such as a school rivalry gone wrong, or war against the employee, employer, town, politic, institution, schools of thought, culture, race, or other social constructs, maybe religion, which seems a popular reason to crush a family, such as show a slight variation, a minor expression of freedom, which at the wrong time causes a person to be treated as a thing or an it.

And as long as the earth keeps that ugly mess to themselves, yet it now broadcasts on all known channels. As this advanced equipment, timing, and tree have a special broadcast ability, tremendous in fact, especially subspace domains, which might contain a near unlimited number of channels, places, and into potential retreats, havens, sanctuaries and enclaves. While some sit nested within other things, such as counter-enclaves, second-order enclaves, counter-counter-enclave and third-order enclave, and some even have an extraterritoriality aspect to them. And they might sit protected from chaos, from restless churn, cruel and unusual, from destruction, which tends to devalue goodwill, intellect, charm and wit, until the system becomes a crude literary trope.

So here and now these people poke the beasts, with a special ultimate high stakes brinkmanship effort, with a major breach in social protocol, which might serve as an SOS, or finally showcase the earth, reveal the location.

And this broad spectrum transmission into the universe, this message into so many channels, as well as subspace and hidden domains, and interrupting so many systems without warning or permission, well, it represents bad manners, a new form of escalation, plus draws a considerable attention to the planet, which is already in enough trouble, already at war with every known social construct.

And there are certain alien species that expect peace and quiet, not someone polluting the airwaves with nonsense; not that music is inherently such.

Because, well, it can be quite nice, at least to some people.

In fact music from a golden age seems difficult to dispute; however, not everyone agrees with any given golden age.

Here and now, this old-school preacher—known for hellfire in-your-face sermons as if at war and take no prisoners, of bible-thumping, Old Testament fury, known for considering dancing and singing of all types unequivocally immoral, begins to tap his foot, tap his trademark hillbilly boot.

Then moments later, the preacher finds a full accord with nature and dances in front of the tree, yes, that tree.

Elsewhere, at the churches, and one after another, toddlers, then kids begin to dance, as the music compels.

And each of them steps into full accord then invites everyone to join in, other kids, adults, stuffy church officials, even one passerby after another.

In fact, the toddlers turn to the world in general and invite everyone, this means you, whether you sit in an office cubicle, movie theater, dinner table, stand in front of your stern boss, sit in a boardroom meeting, listen to your parents scold you regardless of your age, or you stand ready to execute a trade on the stock market floor, regardless, come alive, really alive, and dance that first song, "a long way from home," well, to open a golden age.

And adults look at the kids, wonder, heads shake with *Woe is me!*

Then one by one, they abandon protocol and join the celebration.

They dance, which include Baptist, Catholic, and Lutheran.

Then a nearby Buddhist monk finds bliss, finds a slow universal wave in ritualized space, which has all those benefits and natural harmony of an ever so smooth transition.

And moments later, nearby town folks hear, turn, and dance.

They celebrate.

Even grannies and eventually grandpops join.

Immediately after, two more songs play, which a person might mistake for the original "Rollin' and Tumblin'" by R.L. Burnside and "I Got a Woman" by Jimmy McGriff with Bonnie on the organ.

Yet the band seems unwilling to leave, and that often happens in a show, the atmosphere feels right and ever so true.

So abandoning it now feels abrupt, and not a natural time to pause, not at a natural lull, well, before the next segment or branch begins, if any.

As a result, Bonnie sings "I'll Be Back Someday", as if Howlin' Wolf, live at the 1964 American Folk Blues Festival.

And some performers do that, completely transform, show another personality, from mild to a voice that roars as if the blues singer Howlin Wolf, in primetime agony and ecstasy, those raw powerful feelings of tenderness as well as bold rough and tumble.

Yet midway through, and with less than ninety seconds to go in that escape window, the music stops, and they rapidly unhook musical equipment, grab weapons and other essentials then bolt in various directions.

En route, the window of safety slams shut as they flee, jump, duck, run, leap, eventually belly crawl, move along a switch back, sprint, wait, jog, shimmy, dart, stop and study at one wait point after another, then run for their lives.

The last to depart, the CIA super wonk, and this person doubles back within seconds yet the memory fades, as this person struggles to continue recording events on a USB drive, which blinks a red recording light.

Meanwhile eyes widen, and this wait to capture as many details as possible causes a fidget, flinch, and slight crouch at every nearby sound then nervous look and lip bite, which anticipates a fate worse than death, while this flash drive continues to save data.

Then in a brief moment of bravado, the wonk says as a serious threat and offers a fist shake, "You have no idea who you're dealing with!" then that moment passes into a shrug, "I fight like a cow."

Elsewhere and as turmoil continues inside those main command bunkers, the Punk Buster seems unflappable, as the backup computer runs painfully slow, and all types of bunker alarms clamor, as more computer firewalls collapse.

Then one deterrent after another goes offline, deterrents that maintain critical worldwide financial market checks and balances, as these routines stave off robber barons.

Then moments later, the critical forest data stream ability stops, the ability to transmit data through five Alcatel-Lucent 7950 XRS style internet routers to satellites, which disperse into the media as well as financial markets.

And all the while that backup computer system runs painfully slow, as the creature fixates on her, on Bonnie, and not on all that turmoil, that *coup d'état* within the underground system, all that extreme confusion, commotion, agitation, polarization, and threat of internal destruction.

Then the fixation translates into a fully absorbed mental loop of immense frustration, smolder, stare, agitation, indignation, spite and thoughts of a pernicious revenge against her, the Mighty Sparrow, a woman who refuses to surrender as the computer system plays that song, "Ye banks and braes o' bonnie Doon, How ye can bloom so fresh and fair, How can ye chant ye little birds, And I sae weary fu' o' care, Ye'll break my heart ye warbling birds, That wantons thro' the flowering thorn, Ye mind me o' departed joys, Departed never to return."

# About The Author

Born in Princeton, New Jersey, Bryan Fletcher is a science fiction, adventure nerd or geek who combines deep insight in one field of study after another to create the ultimate survivor genre, especially a hero against all odds, against powerful special interests too big to fail, a system controlled by ultimate insiders who often seem hell-bent on trivial pursuit, obsession, the last war, escalation, plus cruel and usual, as well as world economic domination to create a brave new world, another dystopia, and frequently based on life controlled by big money and massive institutions.

So we live according to them, their concerns or lack of, that style of raising a family, and a system without substantial peer review checks and balances, those vital safe features, and those vital aspects to live a cool, calm, and reasonable life.

The system seems dominated by big money and massive institutions, which often experiment beyond rhythm or reason and rush into one quagmire after another, which they hype—that hyper style—such as surge into a new version of same old, same old.

In the meantime, they continue to create a new version of the poorhouse for the poor and middle class.

So here we are, Legend of the Mighty Sparrow: Part Three— End of Days, Eschatology, the Final Events of History, the Ultimate Human Destiny, End of Time, and Ultimate Fate of the Universe.